The Man From Darke County

by N. Sullivan

First Print Edition 2014

ISBN: 0692332162

ISBN-13: 978-0692332160 (Sixty Six Underground)

Published by Sixty Six Underground

www.nsullivan.co

To my family, for everything.

To M.C. Shipley

CHAPTER 1

"The phone is ringing. It's five o'clock in the morning. Who's calling at five o'clock in the morning?"

Alan was talking to himself. Alone. In bed. There was no reason for it; there was no one to hear it. He was in bed for godsakes. It was five o'clock in the morning. He should probably stop talking to himself.

The sun was barely even up. No. That wasn't the sun. That was his television. It wasn't even yellow, just kind of a blue grey. Eventually he'd have to find the remote and turn it off. No self-respecting man would

- 1 -

ever walk over to the TV and simply push the button. Why the hell did he think that an infomercial was the sun?

Alan stumbled across the room and grabbed the phone.

"Detective Schriever?" The voice on the other end of the phone sounded like a robot. Who smoked too much. And hadn't had coffee yet. In general, unpleasant.

"Who died?" Alan tried not to sound hungover to the point of possibly still drunk. It was a difficult task when he was wading through a sea of empty liquor bottles trying to remember where he hid his closet. He needed to clean up eventually.

"Uhh, I'm not *sure*, Detective. No one is. But the Captain asked me to call you."

Yep, still a remarkably unpleasant robot. Alan wondered if all uniformed cops had been replaced with unpleasant robots during his time off.

No, that was a stupid idea.

"I'm suspended. Why am I getting called in at five o'clock in the morning?" Alan asked. He looked down at his coffee maker. It was supposed to be in the kitchen, but had apparently decided to take up residence in the hall by the bathroom door. It was plugged in and ready to go. He didn't know why it would want to be in the hall, but it seemed perfectly comfortable there. Best to not disturb it.

Alan was definitely still drunk.

"Uhh, Detective we've come across something... strange. Captain says he wants to talk to you right now." The robot was faltering. It was capable of emotion. Only a matter of time before it decides humanity is a threat and the war begins.

Alan thought he might have hit his head. Or possibly gone insane? Was that an option? It certainly made more sense than a robot takeover of Earth led by generally unpleasant patrolman drones. He really, really needed to sober up.

"Alan." This voice was definitely human, but no happier. "Alan, this is Captain Clark. You're off suspension."

"And to what do I owe this great honor, Captain?" Alan said.

He'd known the Captain for fifteen years, worked under him for the past seven, if you count the last year on suspension. The Captain never liked him, and his *behavior* sealed the deal. He was suspended pending further review. That suspension left him in limbo: he couldn't get hired anywhere else, and he couldn't work as a cop. He's been on half pay this whole time. Lost his house, everything.

Part of him thought that killing the Captain would be a fun way to spend a Wednesday morning. Unfortunately murder was messy, and he kinda wanted to eat breakfast, also, he wanted to see what was so important that the Captain was willing to bring him into the field when he swore Alan would never work again.

"Okay. Give me the address," Alan said, writing the numbers and street name on the mirror in red lipstick. He looked down at the lipstick tube. Whose lipstick was this?

"Schriever, you'd better know this wasn't my choice. This goes way over my head," Captain Clark said.

"I had a feeling it was something like that. Give me an hour. I'll be there," Alan said, turning on the shower.

Twenty minutes later he was ready to leave. His coffee maker had still performed its duty from the new place it had apparently chosen for itself in the hall. It, unlike Alan, was not on suspension.

Alan poured himself a cup. It looked like coffee. Smelled vaguely coffee-like. He tasted it. It was *not* coffee. Something more akin to the anal secretions of an angry Mexican bishop was in his coffee cup. He probably should have washed the coffee filter. Or the pot. Or the cup. Something was definitely dirty. In a very bad way.

He threw the cup out the window. The coffee hit the lawn outside and burst into flames like napalm, starting a fire that might conceivably burn for eternity. At least in his head that's what should have happened. The coffee actually hit the grass with an unimpressive splash, the ceramic cup bouncing off the lawn and flopping about for a moment before settling in to its new existence as a decorative ornament of abject failure in the coffee arts. Alan considered the disappointing turn reality was taking this morning for a moment before rinsing his mouth with something that smelled enough like mouthwash to convince an inattentive observer and heading out the door.

Twenty minutes later he pulled up outside the police tape. He waited in his car for a moment, wondering if he'd turned the coffee maker off. Also, since it was now self-propelling, did he really have the right to turn it off at all, or was that killing a living thing? Also, was the owner of that lipstick still in his house? He hoped they didn't kill his new coffee maker roommate.

Alan got out of his car and flashed his badge at the uniform standing at the tape. She didn't look like an android to him.

There weren't people everywhere. It was quiet on the street. Usually there were at least a few people rubbernecking at a crime scene, but apparently 6 a.m. is too early for the Vienna, Ohio, Gawker Brigade. He saw Captain Clark walking toward him from an alley.

"Alan. How are you?" The Captain said.

Like a tiny troll is swinging his hammer at anything that moves in my head. Like the ground beneath my feet is simply an illusion that could evaporate at any time. "I'm good, Captain. I'm doing better." Alan said. The two men shook hands.

"Good. We've got something strange here. I saw it and thought of you. You always had a taste for... You're crazy." The Captain was leading him down the alley. There were cops and technicians standing all around. All of them with some variation of the same expression on their faces. They varied from severely disgusted to horrified. A large tarp was laid across the alley. It looked a bit like a fallen tent. Everyone seemed to be keeping their distance from it.

The Captain led Alan over to the tarp. He pulled it back and turned his head.

The substance below was a person, at some point. He could see where the eyes went, the teeth, the general outline of what had been an average-sized man. It still looked like a man, but more jelly. Melting jelly. Red and yellow and white, translucent, liquefying jelly.

"Well, that's disgusting," Alan said. "What happened to him?"

"If we knew that, we wouldn't have called in the crazy squad." Johnson had walked up behind them. He had that way of sneaking up even when you could see him coming. Like some weird forensics ninja.

"Hello, Greg." Alan said, trying to hold back the vomit in his throat. He thought it might be bad that the jellied man on the ground didn't make him want to throw up, but seeing Greg Johnson did. Nah, Greg Johnson was way more disgusting than a melty guy.

"Detective Schriever. Did you enjoy your time off?" Johnson asked.

That voice. That snotty little face like an arrogant Pomeranian. The obnoxious way he stood. It all deserved to be ground into the pavement.

Alan didn't like him.

"Any wonderful scientific insights into what could turn a man into translucent jelly, Greg?" Alan asked.

"We won't know anything until we can get him to the lab and do some tests." Greg said.

"In that case, could you back away? You're distracting and making my stomach hurt." Alan said, turning toward the Captain.

"Any ID?" he asked the Captain.

"Yeah, but we can't get to it yet. It's in his back pocket, under him," the Captain said.

"Yeah. I suppose you can't just roll him over. You're gonna need a couple of those big pizza spatulas just to get him in a body bag," Alan poked the corpse with the tip of his shoe. The whole body jiggled, "or a Zip Lock." he turned to no one in particular. "Do they make Zip Locks that big?" he asked.

No one in particular decided not to respond.

"Well, I suppose asking how he died is kind of pointless. Is there a police code for *turned into a jello sculpture of a man*?" Alan said.

"No, no code for that. Also, there's no way to know until we get him to the lab if that's actually what killed him. We don't even know if whatever he's turned into is dangerous." Greg said.

"So he could be radioactive? Infectious? Lemon flavored? Are you sure he's actually dead? He could be some kind of jello zombie, just waiting for the chance to turn us all," Alan asked. Nah, he wasn't lemon flavored. Even a translucent man-shaped pile of jelly was too good for that.

The Captain leaned in and spoke into Alan's ear.

"I'm beginning to think I brought you off sabbatical too early, Detective Schriever," he said.

"I think you might be right," Alan whispered back. "I also think you're standing way too close for this to be appropriate in public. Also, I know something about the victim."

The Captain leaned away from Alan. "What do you know, Detective?"

"Well, I'm pretty sure he's not lemon flavored," Alan said. "I'll be at the office in two hours. Call me if Greg and his unholy minions find anything."

"I can still hear you!" Greg yelled.

"You might be a *robot*!" Alan yelled over his shoulder.

Alan got to his apartment two hours later. He'd driven around for a while, tried to get the feel for being outside again. It wasn't something he was used to anymore. He didn't like to think about it.

He unplugged the coffee maker from the hall. He carried it into the kitchen under his arm. Pushing the dirty dishes aside, he rinsed out the pot. He dug up the scrubber and soap and washed it out. The water came out black. He washed it over and over again until the water finally ran clear. He pulled out the filter, scrubbed out the area underneath it. He cleaned the coffee maker until it was as clean as new. By the time he was done, he felt like the maid of a rich man with OCD.

He ground coffee. Straight from the bean, just like it should be. He got out a new cotton filter. Paper changed the flavor. Unbleached cotton was the only way to drip brew. Even thinking that he felt like a massive nerd.

He listened to the coffee dripping into the pot. Drop after drop of slow drip, premium goodness. He could smell it. It smelled pretty good this time.

Alan went into the bathroom and ran cold water, splashing it in his face. It has been so long, he didn't know if he could to it anymore. He looked at the address scrawled on the mirror. For some reason it felt like it had been months since he wrote that.

The coffee finished. Alan walked back into the kitchen to the wonderful scent of a fresh brew. He poured the coffee into a cup. It smelled beautiful. Better than anything else in his apartment, for sure.

Alan held the cup under his nose, sniffing the aroma, the glorious effervescence. He tipped the cup and took a sip, savoring the bitter, disgusting, almost virulent brutality of the worst thing he had ever tasted. It wasn't even coffee. He couldn't imagine where that brown fluid even came from. It was worse than this morning.

Alan threw the liquid into the sink. The coffee maker just sat there on the counter, blinking its little red light at him, silently laughing.

"Why do you keep doing this to me?" Alan screamed. "I cleaned you, I let you sit in the hall all day, I've been good to you and this is what I get for all that? What have I ever done to deserve this? You are the *worst* roommate I've ever had. I've never been anything but nice to you and you're nothing but a dick to me! I bought you myself, I gave you a home! I don't get it!"

Alan was out of breath. His chest heaved. He was almost seeing red. Then he realized he was arguing with a coffee maker. Why the hell was he arguing with an appliance?

Alan grabbed his keys and walked out.

CHAPTER 2

Four hours later, Alan walked into the office.

"Where have you been?" the Captain asked.

"I, well...   Do you really want the honest answer?" Alan said.

The Captain stared for a moment. "No, I really don't In my office."

Alan followed the Captain into his office and took a seat in front of the desk. The air was stagnant, flat like a three day old pop that hadn't been sealed. It smelled faintly of Old Spice and desperation, if desperation was made of dry cleaning chemicals and alcohol-based markers. That may have just been the Old Spice. Or possibly Alan's internal monologue sucked at analogies.

"We got an ID on the body." the Captain said. He looked at a piece of paper on his desk. "Aaron Burroughs," he said, "twenty-six years old. From Arcanum."

"Arcanum? As in Darke County? That Arcanum?" Alan asked, leaning forward in his chair.

"Yes, *that* Arcanum," the Captain said.

"That whole county is nothing but fake psychics and New Agers who never grew up," Alan said.

The Captain looked over Alan's shoulder.

"That's quite an assumption from a man who thinks the Medical Examiner might be a robot," a voice said.

Alan looked around. It was possible that was the stapler, but how would the stapler know details about the victim like that? It could have read the report when the Captain had it open on his desk, but staplers didn't have eyes. They also didn't have mouths. It wasn't the stapler. Ceiling fan, maybe?

No, most likely the guy sitting behind him in the corner. He was in a black suit. White shirt, black tie. His dark hair was impossibly perfect. His shoes were impossibly shiny. His skin was possibly white. He was sitting in a shadow. It was hard to tell. Maybe Hispanic? Native American? The man in the corner stood up.

"Detective Alan Schriever, meet Detective John Weatherby, Darke County Sheriff's Office," the Captain said.

The two men shook hands. Alan noticed that he was average height, maybe five nine, and average build. He was so average that it was uncanny. Like he was *trying*.

"Nice to meet you, Detective Schriever," Detective Weatherby said.

"Nice to meet you too, Detective Weatherby. Robot?" Alan asked.

"I'm sorry, what?" Detective Weatherby said, his head cocking as his eyes narrowed.

"You two have a lot to go over if you're going to find out what happened," the Captain interrupted Alan before he could clarify his question. "Better get out there."

"Yes, Captain, you're right," Detective Weatherby said. "And thank you for agreeing to keep the circumstances of this under wraps. Until we know what it is, best to keep speculation to a minimum."

"Of course. Thank you for offering to assist. This is really a new one. Shut the door on your way out?" the Captain said, sitting back down in his chair.

The two detectives walked out of the office and through the bullpen. Eyes glanced out under eyebrows at them as they crossed through the room.

"They're staring at you," Alan said.

"Pretty sure they're staring at you, Alan," Detective Weatherby responded.

"Why do you think that?" Alan said.

"Because I'm not the one who just came back from a suspension," Weatherby said.

"Yeah, I guess there's that. I'm not crazy, you know," Alan said.

"Didn't say you were, Alan. Though you did ask me if I was a robot in there, and I'm pretty sure you thought the stapler was talking. I'd like to see the crime scene now. I'll fill you in on the victim in the car," John said.

"Fine with me," Alan said. He wanted to swing by his house first. He still hadn't found the owner of that lipstick, and he was a little worried for the coffee maker, but he figured it could handle itself.

On the way to the scene, John filled Alan in.

"Aaron Burroughs, twenty-six years old. Raised in Darke County, top of his class at MIT, Ph.D. from Cornell in Particle Physics. Returned to Arcanum to be close to family while he continued his research," John said as he navigated the city streets.

"Wow," Alan said, looking over the file, "this guy looks like a real life genius. Probably don't get many of those in Arcanum. Was there anything in his research that could have caused this?"

"We've had our fair share, like anywhere else. I'm not a scientist, so I really couldn't tell you, but turning a body into jelly shouldn't be possible in any physics I've heard of," John said.

Aliens. Could be aliens. Would they do something like this? Nah. Maybe witches? An angry leprechaun's curse? Don't say any of this out loud.

"Maybe a gypsy curse, then?" Alan asked. Damn.

"Honestly, I hope not," John said.

Alan looked at his face. His blue eyes were shaded by Wayfarer sunglasses, but he could see his jaw get tense and his forehead furrow as he thought about the question.

"We're here," John said, parking at the end of the alley.

They hopped out of John's black SUV and walked toward the crime scene tape. A few uniformed patrolmen were still hanging around, guarding the scene, but they were mostly there to drink coffee. Alan wondered why robots enjoyed coffee so much.

"Hey, Mark," Alan said to the patrol droid that had replaced Mark, "he's with me." Alan gestured to John and the patrol droid lifted the crime scene tape.

Once they'd crossed under he stopped for a moment to marvel at the craftsmanship of the droid's face. Mark gave him a funny look.

"This is where they found him?" John asked. He had walked ahead a short distance and stopped at a wet looking spot in the alley.

"Yeah. That's it. Looks like there's still... Bits," Alan said.

John pulled a small box out of his pocket. It had a meter on the front with a switch and a dial. He flipped the switch and fiddled with the dial a bit. The needle jumped back and forth.

"What's that?" Alan asked.

"Electromagnetic field detector. Like I said, I'm not a scientist, but I know Burroughs was working in electromagnetics. If his work did cause this, it might have left a trace," John said.

He moved the detector over the melting chunks of Aaron Burroughs that the coroner had left in the alley.

The meter didn't seem to move around much, as far as Alan could tell. He wasn't really paying attention. He was wondering whose job it would be to rinse the leftovers into the gutter when they were all done with the scene.

John had moved away from the area where the body was found to the adjacent wall. He scanned up the wall, moving the detector back and forth until he couldn't reach any higher.

"What is this building?" John asked.

"The first couple floors are stores and offices, above that are lofts," Alan said.

"Okay, I'm done here. You ready to go see the M.E.?" John asked.

"Ready when you are," Alan said, staring blankly at the roof tops on either side of the alley.

They got back in the SUV and drove to the Medical Examiner's office.

Alan didn't like the M.E.'s office. Never had. It was cold. Dim yet somehow gleaming white. Everything stank of industrial cleaner yet seemed dingy. Plus, the bodies were kept in the basement. They had the whole building all to themselves. Four stories of offices and presumably robot repair facilities for damaged city employees, and they kept the dead people in the basement. That was creepy. Why the basement? It was like they were trying to hide the fact that there were dead bodies *in the morgue*. They would all be underground soon enough. He was sure some of them would appreciate a little better view for now.

Greg was there, sitting behind his desk, eating a sandwich. Morose, humorless, no-imagination Greg. He was a doctor of some kind; Alan always assumed it was a Ph.D. Probably philosophy. Or English. He had that *nothing to live for* look in his glassy eyes; that stank of an English degree, or, of course, being a robot. But to be fair, most robots probably had advanced degrees in English.

Speaking of stinking, what was that sandwich? It looked like maybe meat of some kind. Pimento loaf? Slathered in a disgusting sauce that could have come from Alan's coffee maker. Alan realized Greg was talking.

"Honestly, I have no idea what killed him. I can't exactly put *turned into jelly* on a death certificate. Any help you could give me could make this investigation go a lot easier," Greg said, looking at Detective Weatherby.

"Have you checked the body for radiation? He was a physicist, so he may have been experimenting with something dangerous," John said.

"I haven't yet, but I can," Greg said. He looked at his sandwich, the tiny pimentos staring back at him. Greg shrugged and carried the sandwich with him to the door.

He led them through a couple of hallways and into the morgue. Detective Weatherby paused at the door and crossed himself before following Alan and Greg in. He joined Alan at a small table covered in dust masks and boxes of rubber gloves.

"Religious?" Alan asked.

"Respectful," John said. "I was raised to not ever take death lightly."

The two men joined Greg at an exam table in the middle of the room.

"Normally," Greg said, "it would be a while before we could get to a body when there's no sign of foul play but given the, uhh, circumstances, I figured this should get priority."

"You thought right," Weatherby said. He pulled the electromagnetic field detector out of his coat and ran it over the jellied corpse that was once Aaron Burroughs, but was now slowly melting into the table and dripping into the drain below like a piece of birthday cake wetted by melting ice cream.

Greg excused himself while he went to find a radiation detector.

"John, if this guy might be radioactive, should we be this close to him?" Alan asked.

"If he was dangerously radioactive, it would have set off the sensors when they brought him in the building. All government buildings are fitted with radiation detectors now," John said.

"I must have missed that briefing. Hey, I've been wondering something. Why that alley? He lived in Arcanum. That's an hour away from here. I know people come in for a night on the town or a dinner or whatever, but that area isn't exactly entertainment central. It's mostly run down factories and tenements. What was he doing there?" Alan asked.

"I've been asking myself the same question. I think finding that answer might be the key to this whole thing. Here, look at this," John pointed to the EMF detector's meter. "Those are the same as the readings I was getting on the wall in the alley." John said.

"I found the Geiger counter," Greg said. "Let's see what we have."

He turned the machine on and ran it over the body. Alan listened to the clicks. Syncopated, rhythmically out of focus. They were a strange alien language, ticking out their words of warning to an uncomprehending world. Also, it was measuring radiation.

"Nothing," Greg said, turning off the machine. "Everything is well within limits."

Alan noticed that Greg hadn't acknowledged him once this whole time. He leaned over to John. "Can you see me?"

"Yes, I can see you," John said.

"Can *he* see me?" Alan asked, nodding at Greg.

"I can see you just fine, Detective Schriever," Greg interjected, "I'm just choosing to talk to Detective Weatherby because he's not dangerously insane."

Alan stared at his feet. "I'm not dangerous," he said under his breath.

"What is really unusual, though, is what I found when I took a look at whatever the hell he's made of under a microscope," Greg said. "It's seriously not like anything I've ever seen, totally different."

He had a smile on his face. He was standing over a body with a pimento loaf sandwich and a grin. People thought Alan was crazy, they should see this guy at work. Johnson walked over to the microscope, beckoning the two detectives to join him.

"Usually when I do this," he said, "I have a pretty good idea what I'm going to see. This time, well…"

He turned on the microscope light and fiddled with the focus nobs.

"Look at this," he said, leaning away from the eyepieces.

John stepped forward and leaned in, looking through the eyepieces himself.

"Huh, that is weird. Alan, have a look," John said.

Alan stepped forward. He put his eyes to the eyepieces and saw exactly what he expected to: Nothing he understood in the least.

"I don't see anything," he said.

"Exactly," Greg said. "There should be something. Cells, membranes, all sorts of things that are in the flesh. There's none of it."

Alan looked at Greg. He looked scared. Honestly white in the face. He'd seen Greg examine the bodies of dead children without so much as an uncomfortable look in his eye. Greg had seen more horror than any cop on the force, yet this one sample turned him white.

"Maybe you got a bad sample?" Alan asked.

"Alan," Detective Weatherby said, "all flesh has that stuff. Literally everything alive has it in one form or another. It's impossible to have a bad sample."

Alan looked again at the two men. One trying to look like he's not some kind of creature of the night in witness protection, the other a poorly designed and kind of glitchy robot. Both of them seriously freaked out.

"Doctor," John said, "there's nothing you can think of that could cause anything like that?"

"Honestly, no. There's nothing I've ever seen that could cause that in anything. It's actually impossible. It's like some kind of magic," Greg said.

"There's no such thing as magic, Doctor," John said.

Alan and John left him there, staring through the eyepieces at something inexplicable. Alan thought the alien thing might be right after all. It was the best theory he had.

John slipped on his Wayfarers before opening the door to the street. He stood there for a moment on the sidewalk, staring at the police station across the street. Alan stepped up beside him

"John, what the hell is going on?" he asked.

"I don't know yet," John said, "but I think you're right about that alley. Something about him being there is strange. I met Dr. Burroughs a few times since he came back. He was straight laced, a classic scientist. There was no reason for him to be there in the middle of the night."

The two men stared at the building. Alan thought it looked a little fat from this angle.

"I know a guy," John interrupted Alan's thought. "He grew up in Darke County. A career criminal from a family of criminals. Now he lives here. He still has a lot of connections back home. Our little community is pretty tight. If Aaron Burroughs was up to anything he shouldn't have been this guy would know about it."

"How do we find him?" Alan asked.

"We won't yet. You'll never catch him out during the day. I'll check back with my contacts and find out where he's prowling these days. Meet me at the station around seven?" John turned to Alan and extended his hand.

"Seven it is," Alan said, shaking John's hand.

Alan crossed the street and headed into the station.

CHAPTER 3

It didn't take Alan nearly as long to get home this time. He drove straight there. It wasn't because he was particularly interested in getting home; he just didn't want to be outside anymore.

Outside meant dealing with stares, people second guessing him on everything, and overhearing comments. Also the sun, crowds, and the remote-yet-distinct possibility that his theories about a robot takeover led by semi-intelligent police drone are true, and in that case, home is a much safer place to be.

He walked into the hall. There was the coffee maker next to the bathroom door, right where he didn't leave it. He'd left half a pot of coffee in it, now it was empty. Also, it was back in the hall.

He walked into the bathroom, figuring another shower might be in order, or at least a freshening up. He could still smell the morgue on his shirt. It smelled like cleanser. Not the fresh scent of a name brand laundry detergent, not even the manly scent of a good bar soap. Just ammonia, bleach, and death. Also, a little bit of pimento loaf. That sandwich really stunk.

Something was different in the bathroom. He looked around, even checking in the mirror to see if he had changed when he wasn't looking. He needed a haircut. Also, the writing he'd put on the mirror was gone. Someone had cleaned his mirror, wiping it down and removing the address. They hadn't even had the common decency to make sure to leave it with a streak-free shine.

Alan looked at the sink. The lipstick tube he'd use to write the note in the first place was gone. Not on the floor, not in the sink, not in the trash can. He reached for his gun. No gun. No gun for months. Damn. He could really use a gun. Now all those NRA ads made sense.

"Was this you?" Alan said, leaning out the door and looking at the coffee maker.

The machine just blinked its little red light at him, mocking his attempt at interrogation. God, his coffee maker was a dick. He figured that the coffee maker was responsible for this. Nothing else made sense. No one had come in, nothing was moved, nothing was stolen. Everything was exactly as it had been, except for the lipstick on the mirror, and the coffee maker, and the missing lipstick tube. He hadn't given a key to anybody, and he kept the door locked when he wasn't home. It just didn't make sense.

Alan went back into the bathroom and splashed water on his face. After he'd dried off with what appeared to be the cleanest towel, he went to the bedroom and changed his suit.

At six forty-five, Alan was sitting in the bullpen, waiting for John. He felt out of place here now. It had been six months since he last sat at one of these desks, a fully-functioning member of the Major Crimes Unit. Grinding away on the worst crimes that the city had to offer, and doing a damn good job at it.

Now he stood. He had no desk, no gun. He barely had a badge, and even that was temporary. He knew that the Captain was hoping he'd fail. The only reason he hadn't been fired was union rules. If he was ill and could be cured, they had to keep him on. If he was ill and couldn't be cured, they had to give him his pension. They didn't want to do either of those. They wanted to fire him, which they could only do if he screwed up and showed incompetence or some other specifically fireable offense. He hadn't committed one, so they were stuck with him until he did.

People were glancing up at him. Nervous eyes peering from around computer screens, looking out under worried brows that gave the distinct impression of mildly medicated owls caught in the middle of taking a dump on the side of the road. He didn't wonder anymore why criminals knew they were being watched. These cops were terrible at it. They had all the stealth of five-year-olds waiting for Santa Claus and none of the cuteness.

"Hey," Detective Weatherby said. He had walked up behind Alan as he watched the other cops doing their worst impersonations of sneaky prairie dogs. "Are you ready to go?"

"What? Yeah. Where are we going?" Alan asked.

"I got a tip on the guy I was looking for. I know where he's going to be tonight," John said.

"Okay," Alan said, "you can fill me in on the way."

"Wait," John said. "Before we go, I have something for you." He reached into the back of his pants and pulled out Alan's pistol.

Try not to smile try not to smile try not to smile.

"They're giving me my gun back?" Alan asked, smiling.

"Yeah. I talked to your Captain earlier today. I explained that until we knew who or what we were dealing with, it wasn't a good idea to have you going around unarmed," John said.

"And he bought that?" Alan asked, checking his gun.

"Well, there may have been a bit of strong-arming," Detective Weatherby said, smiling.

Alan smiled back. How did Weatherby strong arm the Captain? He was one of the most unshakable men Alan had ever known.

Just then the Captain walked by. He nodded his head at Alan, then looked at John. The Captain looked down as he passed John, refusing to make eye contact. *Who was this guy?*

John clapped his hand on Alan's shoulder, still smiling. "Come on, let's go," he said.

Alan clipped his gun onto his belt and followed Weatherby out to his SUV.

CHAPTER 4

Half an hour later they were parked on the side of the road in the warehouse district.

"So," John said, "this is the guy we're looking for." He handed Alan a dossier. "He's from one of the newer families in Darke County. They go back to the Victorian era."

"That's one of the newer families?" Alan asked. He looked at the picture in the street light. The man was about average size, maybe a little thinner. There wasn't a mug shot, just a surveillance photo, but Alan could see his sharp jaw and high cheekbones. His eyes were small and keen, and his body was leaning forward a little, as though ready to run at any moment.

"Why do you think he'll know what's going on?" he asked John.

"He's careful, very careful. He makes it his business to know everything he can to make sure he doesn't get caught up in it," John said.

He was looking out the windshield. His eyes had narrowed as he stared up the dark street. The light was dim, hard to see anything clearly, but as John stared through the glass, Alan saw a slight glimmer in his eyes, like the reflection when you shine a flashlight at a cat at night. Or maybe just a normal reflection from the street lamp? Was Alan's partner actually a cat? Probably not. Alan pondered on whether a cat-man or a robot would make a worse partner.

"There he is," John said, breaking Alan's now entirely derailed train of thought.

Alan looked up the street. A block away, just now coming into view, was the man in the picture. He was wearing a hooded sweatshirt and jeans. He looked more the part of a low level drug dealer than a paranoid master criminal who kept his ear to the ground.

Alan watched as the man walked up the other side of the street. He was watching them, too. He was trying too hard not to look at them. He knew they were there.

"Why don't you talk to him?" Weatherby said.

"Me?" Alan responded. "Why me?"

"He knows me, and he'll bolt as soon as I get close. He'll think you're just trying to figure out what he's doing here at night," John said.

"Where will you be?" Alan asked.

"I'll be nearby. He's not violent, but he is quick," John said, a tiny smile creasing the corner of his mouth.

"Okay, then," Alan said, stepping out of the SUV.

"Hey, buddy. Police. Hold on a second," Alan said, showing his badge and trying to sound authoritative and not at all like a robot or a crazy guy.

The man stopped in front of an alley between a two story warehouse and a much taller manufacturing building. "What can I do for you officer?" he asked, looking Alan over.

"What are you doing out here so late?" Alan asked.

"Just going for a walk. It's a free country, isn't it?" The man's posture was loose, but he kept stepping backward toward the alley.

"That's what I hear. I've got a couple questions for you," Alan said.

The man looked up and down the street and stepped back into the alley.

Why an alley? Why did he have to do that? Alleys are dark and bad things happen in them. This was going to be like American Werewolf in London.

"Ask away, Detective. I've got nothing to hide," the man said, looking up at the buildings on either side.

"You're from Darke County. You know a guy by the name of Aaron Burroughs?" Alan asked.

The man's eyes widened.

"Nope!" he said. "No way," the man jumped straight up in the air. Alan watched as he gained altitude exactly like a human didn't. In the blink of an eye, he was on the roof of the two story building. Then, just as quickly, he was hanging in mid-air over the ledge in exactly the way Wile E. Coyote did.

Alan watched the man dangle in space. What, exactly, was he? The jump was bad enough, but now he was floating. Could robots float? Nah. That was crazy. They were way too heavy. Maybe it was a gypsy curse after all? He didn't look like a gypsy. No bangles hanging from his head scarf. No head scarf.

"Hey, Schriever!" a voice yelled from the same space the man was hanging in. "Want to come up here and interrogate our suspect?"

It was Weatherby. On the roof. How did Weatherby get on the roof so fast? Also, why was Weatherby on the roof?

"Okay. I'm on my way," Alan yelled back. He found the door on the street unlocked. After a couple minutes he found the stairs and took them up to the roof. He walked through the door to find John and the man, who was now handcuffed to a pipe.

"Took you long enough," John said.

"Yeah, well, I didn't get the super fluoride in my water when I was a kid, I guess," Alan said.

"What?" the man handcuffed to the pipe said.

"And you!" Alan said, pointing at the man as he walked over. "What kind of gypsy doesn't wear a bangled head scarf?"

The man looked at Detective Weatherby. "Seriously, what is he talking about?"

"Alan, I'd like you to meet Springheel Jack. The greatest cat burglar alive," Weatherby said.

"Never heard of him," Alan said.

"Of course not," Springheel Jack said. "I wouldn't be the greatest if I got caught, would I?"

"Jack, this is Alan, he's my partner," John said.

"Why does he think I'm a gypsy?" Jack asked.

"Really not sure," John said. "Now, what do you know about Aaron Burroughs?"

"I can't talk about that, Detective. It's really out of my league. I'm just a cat burglar. I don't hurt people," Jack said.

"You haven't, but you've got it in you to, and we both know it," John said.

"You aren't seriously still holding that against us, are you?" Jack asked.

"What's going on?" Alan asked. He felt like the friend invited to Thanksgiving who had no idea what the family was arguing about.

John turned to Alan. "Jack here has some pretty nasty characters in his family tree. That's the whole reason his family left England," he turned back to Jack. "Isn't it, Jack?"

"Dad's grandpa might have gotten a little bad in the head and a taste for nasty in Whitehall, yeah. But you know the Springheel Jacks have been straight since then," Jack said.

"John," Alan said, "why does any of this matter? Also, are you saying his great grandfather was Jack the Ripper?"

"Yeah," Jack said, "brought terrible trouble to the Springheel Jack lineage."

Alan thought about the boring turn reality had taken this morning. The coffee maker, the coffee not exploding, no talking stapler or ceiling fan. Now, a guy who could jump two stories was a descendant of Jack the

Ripper. After a disappointing morning, reality had finally come through for him.

"You know how the sins of the father don't follow the son?" John asked Alan. "Well, in Darke County, they do. So Jack here has to remember that Great Grandpa Jack's crimes are still attached to his family," he said.

"Except in your case," Jack said, looking at Detective Weatherby, "it's not your father; it's the sins of your mother that matter, isn't it?"

John wrapped his fingers around Jack's neck and squeezed. His lips seemed to peel back into an animal snarl, white teeth gleaming like fangs in the moonlight. "Do I need to remind you who my mother was?" he asked, his smooth voice deepening into an almost inhuman growl.

"Okay, okay. I'm sorry," Jack sputtered.

Weatherby held him for a moment longer, staring into him while his teeth glistened in the light looking every bit like fangs.

"Now," Weatherby said, "tell us what you know about Aaron Burroughs."

"Okay, I will," Jack turned to Alan. "Your new partner's a maniac. You know that, right?"

Alan shrugged his shoulders. "At least he's not a robot," he said.

Jack stared at Alan, his head cocked to the side and mouth slightly open.

"Tell us what you know." John commanded.

"I don't really know much. I swear. But there's somebody throwing parties for us in Vienna," Jack said.

"Us, who?" John asked.

"Members," Jack said

"Members of what?" Alan asked.

"The Darke County Social Club. The Founding Families started it a hundred years ago as a place to meet and discuss their business in private," John said.

"Yeah. Someone is holding parties for them here. Invitation only," Jack said.

"Why would someone hold parties here? There are plenty of places in Darke County for that," John asked.

"Not like this. At these parties, you can do anything you want." Jack looked at Alan, then back at John. "You don't have to obey the club's rules."

"So, these are like underground raves?" Alan asked. He felt like there was a lot more being said here than he was hearing. It was like high school chemistry all over again.

"No, man. Not like raves," Jack said, smiling. "Seriously, Detective Weatherby. Where did you find this guy?"

"In an asylum," John said. "Where are they holding the parties?" he asked.

"I don't know. I think they move around. Nobody knows. Some guys I know have been to them.

They said they got the invitation, then they got taken to the party," Jack said.

"You've never been to one?" John asked.

"Come on, Detective. I'm just a burglar. You know I don't get into…" he looked at Alan again, "stuff."

Yep, just like high school. Not chemistry class anymore. Just high school in general.

"Who's running the parties?" Alan asked.

"I don't know," Jack said, "but whoever he is, the people I know who've gone don't know him. He's not a local at all. No one recognizes him."

"What does this have to do with Aaron Burroughs?" Alan asked.

"Good question," John said. "Tell the man, Jack."

Jack looked at John. "Well somebody mentioned him asking around, being real sneaky telling people he wanted to talk to the guy who ran the parties. It stood out when I heard it, because…"

He looked at Alan again.

"Because he didn't get into that stuff either?" John asked.

Springheel Jack nodded.

"That's all you know?" John asked.

"I swear that's it, Detective. Can you uncuff me now? I have to get back to work," Jack said.

Detective Weatherby unlocked the handcuff on Jack's wrist. Jack turned to jump, but Weatherby caught his collar.

"Don't wander too far, Jack. I might need you again, and you know I can find you," he said.

He let go of Jack's collar and the burglar jumped off the roof and landed in the alley below.

Alan watched as Jack landed gracefully on the pavement then took off running down the street.

"Huh," Alan said.

"What?" John asked.

"Well, I've seen a lot of people get on roofs. I've seen them climb ladders, trees, even up the side of buildings. But I've never seen one jump. Also, I've never seen one jump off a two story building and take off running," Alan said.

"Yeah," John said.

"You're not doing a whole lot for my mental health, John," Alan said.

"I suppose I'm not. Let's get back down to the truck, and I'll explain everything," John said.

The two men walked in silence back to the SUV. Alan had a bad feeling. It wasn't gypsy curse or robots bad; it wasn't even jello zombie bad. Alan had a feeling he was about to find out something much, much more disturbing was going on.

They got in the truck and John started the engine. Pulling away from the curb, Weatherby broke the silence.

"So…" he said.

"Go on," Alan said, turning in his seat to look at John.

"What do you know about Darke County?" John asked.

"I know its west of here. I know you have an absurdly low crime rate, no houses ever go up for sale, there used to be an Army base there, and I know that freaky crap happens all the time" Alan said.

"Well, that's all true. But there's much more to it," John said, looking at Alan.

Alan motioned for him to continue.

"During the Revolutionary War, the American side was looking for any advantage it could get. They turned to a group of ten families who were living on the frontier. Families with a specific… skill set," John said.

"Like assassins? Were they ninjas? That would make this story awesome." Alan said, suddenly excited.

"No, not ninjas or any other kind of assassins. They were witches." John said.

"I would have preferred ninjas." Alan said.

"Anyway," John said, "Captain William Darke knew about these families through his own dealings with the frontiersmen he traded with. When the war was looking bleak, he went to them for help."

"And they agreed?" Alan asked.

"Yes, on the conditions that they would never be named and that they would be allowed to live in peace and secrecy after the war. America wasn't a safe place for witches back then. Darke agreed, and the families used their considerable power to help the rebels turn the tide against the British. After the war, Darke was true to his word and made sure that the government set aside the families' lands and a large area around them as a permanently protected place. It was listed as a county, but in reality was more like a reservation, answering only to the federal government. When Darke died, they reincorporated the county with his name in memoriam," John said.

"So Darke County is a witch reservation?""

"Well, that's how it started out. Over the years, its status as a safe place spread among the persecuted of the world. Everyone from occultists to genetic mutants to fringe scientists call it home now. Only the magic families and other… for lack of a better term, *supernatural* people can join the Social club. The scientists and other outsiders are strictly unwelcome," John said.

"So, the people reading Tarot cards in the square in Arcanum…" Alan said.

"Are hustling you," John said. He cracked a small smile. "Tarot cards aren't *real*."

"Huh. So if Burroughs was looking for access to these parties, he would have been straight up denied" Alan was staring out the windshield. Squinting into the partial darkness of the city streets as buildings rolled past.

"He should have been. There's no reason that parties specifically for magic users would ever invite a physicist. They're kinda looked down upon," John said.

"I have one question," Alan said.

"You've already had five, but go on," John responded.

"Where are we going now?" Alan asked.

As John looked at Alan, his brows furrowed. His perfect hair stayed perfect.

"The police station. I have to make some phone calls to get us in to Aaron Burroughs' house tomorrow," John said.

"Makes sense to me. Maybe we'll find something that links him to those parties," Alan said.

"That's what I'm thinking," John said. He pulled the SUV up to the sidewalk outside the station. There were several patrolmen standing around outside looking bored.

Alan hopped out of the truck and shut the door.

CHAPTER 5

The next morning, Alan woke up to something in his kitchen. It couldn't be the coffee maker; that was still in the hall. Couldn't be burglars. He didn't have anything worth stealing, and everyone in the neighborhood knew it. This actually sounded like someone moving dishes around. Like somebody... Washing his dishes?

He rolled out of bed and grabbed his gun. He didn't know what he'd need the gun for. Anyone willing to do his dishes probably deserved a medal, not to be shot. As he passed the coffee maker in the hall he caught an aroma of fresh-brewed goodness. Whoever this mystery person was, they'd convinced his coffee maker to produce something other than Catholic anal secretions. Now he did kinda want to shoot them. And his coffee maker, just for being a dick.

As he turned the corner into his kitchen, he saw something unlike anything he'd seen in months: His counter, gleaming and clean. The floor was completely bereft of food stains and trash bags. His dishes were in the dry sink. Scarier than that, he'd never realized he had a dry sink.

In the middle of all this horrifying order stood a man. His back was turned. He was wearing yellow rubber gloves. His white dress shirt sleeves were rolled up to the elbows. A full length apron hung over the whole affair.

"Can I help you?" Alan said.

The man turned around. It was John. He had a plate in one hand and a towel in the other. Both hands were busily engaged in the act of drying the plate.

"Oh, good morning, Alan. I knocked, but you didn't answer. When I tried the knob it was open, so I figured I'd start coffee. Then I saw your kitchen and," he gestured around the room, "I guess one thing led to another."

"How long have you been here?" Alan asked, rubbing his eyes.

"Oh, maybe half an hour," John said.

"You did all this in half an hour?" Alan asked, rubbing his eyes again. He wasn't so much trying to rub the sleep out of them as try to cause pain and wake himself up from what was surely a fever dream. It was weird, he didn't feel sick.

"Yeah, did I go too far?" John asked.

"No, not at all. Though I can't guarantee that the monsters in my other dreams won't get jealous that you've put so much effort into scaring the crap out of me. They tend to stick to the standard stuff, like pantsing me in public or growing giant clown heads and attacking me with spiked avocados. Sometimes they become Republicans with veto power if they really want to scare me. You, you've taken it to a whole other level," Alan said.

"Alan, you're not asleep," John said.

Alan focused as best he could. It felt real. His gun was cold in his hand. He pinched himself. It hurt. Damn.

"So, not a dream then?" Alan asked.

"No, not a dream," John answered.

"I should put on pants?" Alan asked.

"I'd prefer it," John said.

Alan waked back to his bedroom, past the bathroom and the coffee maker to the bedroom. He slipped on underwear, a pair of dress pants and a t-shirt and walked back to the kitchen.

John was sitting at the kitchen table. Alan took the seat across from him and stared at the table for a few seconds.

"Did I upset you?" John asked.

"What? No," Alan said. "I just forgot I had this table."

John looked at him for a minute before smiling and taking a sip of his coffee.

He still had his shirt sleeves rolled up. Alan could see that his lower arms were covered in black tattoos. Just from the fragment he could see it looked like a mixture of symbols and writing he couldn't read. Some of it was Latin, but other parts looked like Arabic and Hebrew. Some of it looked like squiggles.

John noticed him looking and started to roll down his sleeves.

"Do those have something to do with magic? Some kind of protection?" Alan asked.

John finished rolling down his sleeves. "Yeah, most of them. We're going to Arcanum today. Burroughs' neighbor is going to let us into his house. I called last night and let them know we're coming," he said.

"Do you think we're going to find anything there?" Alan asked, taking a sip of his coffee. It was very good coffee.

"I don't know," John said, leaning back in his chair, "when one of our people dies, the Council comes in and takes all their research and notes to the archives. It's a way to protect it from prying eyes."

"Why is it such a danger? I mean, doesn't everyone there already know the secret?" Alan asked.

"Oh, yes. Everyone who lives there does. But after Project Rainbow, the Council felt it needed to take further measures to protect our people." John said.

"Project Rainbow?" Alan asked.

"It was a government project during World War II. They were trying to perfect teleportation," John said.

"Teleportation? Seriously?" Alan asked.

"Yeah. Just imagine what they could have done. Being able to drop entire battalions right into Berlin. Spies who could pop in and out without the need for extraction teams. They just appear where they need to be, get the information, and disappear," John said.

"So, what happened?" Alan asked.

"Well, the project failed completely. According to what I heard pretty much every attempt ended with someone dying. What happened next was the worst part, though," John said.

"What, did they shoot everyone involved?" Alan asked.

"No. They came in, collected all the research and redacted the people involved," John said.

"Redacted them? What, did they erase their lives or something?" Alan asked.

"Worse than that. They destroyed all of their research and any documentation showing they had worked for the government and forced them all to sign documents to make them keep quiet. This wasn't just government scientists, either. There were magic users and occultists working on this, too," John said. "Burroughs' grandparents were among the scientists who stayed. They'd been working there for three years, and couldn't explain their absence from the scientific community during the war. They had nowhere to go."

"So, the government disavowed knowledge of a project that was dangerous and failed. They do that all the time. Why was this such a big deal?" Alan asked.

"Yeah, they do. But they didn't have to help. Darke County is exempted from military service. Those people chose to help. Remember, some of them had actually escaped from Nazi Germany just a few years before. The government responded by burning their research and denying all knowledge of them. They shut them down, destroyed their work, and blocked them out."

"That is a *dick move*," Alan said.

"So, in response, the Council decided that all records of work done in Darke County would be stored at the county archives, out of reach of the government, and that Darke County would never aid the Federal Government again," John said.

"So, we're hoping the work isn't in the archives," Alan said.

"More or less. It will be easier to study if they haven't moved it yet," John said.

"I'll be out in a few minutes," Alan said, walking back to his bathroom.

CHAPTER 6

An hour later, they pulled up in front of Aaron Burroughs' house. It was a small bungalow style building with a white picket fence out front. Nothing particularly special about it. Alan was waiting for the two-point-five kids to come out and start riding down the street on their scooters chased by a happy mongrel dog with a patch of black fur around one eye, but as this wasn't nineteen fifty-five, that probably wouldn't happen.

"This is it," John said, shifting the SUV into park.

The two men got out of the car and walked to the front door. An older woman came out of the house next door and walked toward them.

"Detective Weatherby!" She said, waving. "I have the key for you!"

She stopped when she saw Alan standing next to John. Her eyes narrowed.

"Detective," she said, "Does the Council know you brought an outsider here?"

"Mrs. Morlin, the Council doesn't get a say in police business. You know that. This is my partner, Detective Schriever, from Vienna. Alan, this is Mrs. Morlin. Her husband was a teacher here for years," John said.

"Oh, Vienna! That is a beautiful city. My husband served there years ago. That's where we met."

"Was your husband a police officer?" Alan asked, trying to sound sweet.

"Oh, no, dear. He was in the OSS. British, you know," she said, smiling. "You don't have an Austrian accent," her eyes narrowed again.

"It was nice to see you, Mrs. Morlin. Give your husband my best," John said, opening the door and pulling Alan inside. He shut the door behind them.

"OSS?" Alan asked. "Like, British spies during World War Two OSS?"

"Yep. That OSS," John said, switching on the lights.

"So, exactly how old is Mrs. Morlin?" Alan asked.

"Oh, well over a hundred, I'd guess," John said.

"And how old is her husband?" Alan asked.

"Is or was. No one's sure if he's dead or not," John said.

"And here I was worried about my coffee maker. So what are we looking for?" Alan said.

"It's hard to know. Anything he wrote. A day planner, research papers, anything that might give us an idea of why he was trying to find those parties," John said.

"Speaking of those parties, I'm guessing the whole point of them is to do banned magic or something like that," Alan said.

"It seems like that's exactly the point," John said.

"If this place is here to protect people who use magic, then why is anything banned?" Alan asked.

"Well," John said, "some of it is dark magic. The scary stuff that can come back on you. Hexes, curses, that sort of thing. Some of it is just so dangerous that the council banned it to protect people. Like target shooting in a city. Not technically bad, but really, really dangerous."

"That makes sense. I'll take upstairs. You look around down here," Alan said.

He walked up the narrow staircase to the second floor. There were three doors off the landing. The one in the middle was a bathroom, one was a bedroom and the other was an office. The office had been cleared out. Nothing was left but an empty desk and chair. The bedroom was still intact, but there weren't any papers or notes left around. Not even a book. There was a picture of Burroughs and a woman on the bedside table. She was pretty, with long curly hair past the middle of her back and a warm smile. Alan took the picture back downstairs.

Reaching the bottom of the staircase, he found John in the front hall.

"Any luck?" Alan asked.

"Nothing down here. The Council has already cleared it out," John said. "What about upstairs?"

"No papers, but it looks like Burroughs had a girlfriend, you know her?" he asked, handing John the picture.

"Yeah, I know her. This is Sarah Jackson.," John said.

"Who is she?" Alan asked.

"A witch," John said. "Descended from one of the founding families. I've known her since high school," he said.

"Maybe we should go talk to her," Alan suggested, hearing a twinge in John's voice.

John looked up from the photo. "No, not yet anyway. The Council took all his papers; we'll have to go get permission to go into the archive. Let's do that first," he said.

John set the picture down on the hall table. Alan waited in the SUV while John returned the key to Mrs. Morlin.

Alan looked at the house they'd just searched. It was a bungalow. Short, squat little building that looked like it belonged in a beachside resort. Two large front windows on either side of the door that made it look very shocked to see you. More importantly, it was a bungalow, a one story building. *How did he go upstairs?*

John opened the door and slid into the driver's seat.

"John," Alan said, "what happened to Mr. Morlin?"

"Oh. He disappeared," John said, starting the engine.

"Was there an investigation?" Alan asked.

"No, there wasn't a need for one," John said.

Alan looked at him, trying to figure out which form of confusion to express. He finally settled on not knowing that, either.

"He disappeared, Alan. We didn't need to investigate because he walked into a council meeting, said 'I will return when I'm needed' and disappeared, literally," John said.

"So, like *The Once and Future King*?" Alan asked.

"More like that than you realize," John said, pulling away from the curb.

They pulled up in front of the Town Hall a few minutes later. John parked in front of the building and got out of the car, buttoning his black suit jacket and fixing his hair.

"Is it that formal?" Alan asked.

"For me, it is. The Council is very old school. They can turn you away for something as simple as not liking your tie," John said, adjusting the knot on the aforementioned silk noose.

"That doesn't sound like a very efficient way to run a bureaucracy," Alan said.

"If this were a bureaucracy, or a democracy, it wouldn't be. Like I said; the Council is very old school. The members are from the old families, and they're chosen by each other. One representative from each family. Members serve until they die or retire, and then another member of their family is picked to take their place if they haven't named a successor," John said, stepping up onto the curb.

The two men walked toward the building.

"That sounds more like aristocracy than any American form of government" Alan said.

"Also, all the council members are women," John said.

"Another traditional thing?" Alan asked.

"Yeah. The tradition in witch families is that men run businesses and women deal with the other families. There are exceptions, of course, but the Council is an outgrowth of that," John said.

They stopped in front of the doors. Alan checked his reflection, running his fingers through his light hair and fixing his shirt cuffs. He was starting to look older than his years.

"It's amazing that no one from the federal government ever complained," Alan said.

"Oh, there was one senator about ten years ago who tried to make a stink about it," John said, giving his reflection a final check.

"What came of it?" Alan asked.

"His hair fell out," John said, pulling the door open and walking through.

Alan figured he might not want to accuse anyone of being a robot for the next few minutes. But that was okay. His other go-to delusion was witches, and since they all were anyway, they probably wouldn't be insulted. Best not to yell *burn the witch*, though. Just in case.

CHAPTER 7

The Town Hall looked like, well, a town hall. Nothing about it seemed unusual, unless you considered the mythological symbols painted all over the ceilings, but they had that at the Capitol Building in Washington, too. It looked for all accounts like a normal, small town government building that had been in use a lot longer than it should have been, and just retrofitted over the years.

Of course, this building was close to one hundred and fifty years old. Retrofitting included electrical outlets in strange places and the outlines of doorways that had been blocked over and forgotten. There were men and women quietly working away at desks, typing on computers and making notes. Going over paperwork and having coffee. A pretty young woman smiled as she passed him, and Alan turned his head to watch her walk away.

"Pretty, huh?" John said.

"Huh? Oh, yeah. Pretty girl," Alan responded, trying with all his might to speak in words and not the random noises his brain was producing.

"Her name is Liz. I can get her number for you, but it might be bad for your health," John said.

"So I should assume she's some kind of man eating siren or something?" Alan asked.

"No, worse. She's my cousin," John said, grinning.

They came to a security checkpoint. The guard, an older looking, thin black man with intricate patterns of scars along his cheeks, nodded at John, who made small talk. He then took Alan's police credentials and examined them for a solid minute.

"Come on, Larry," John said.

Alan hadn't ever travelled to Africa. He didn't have first-hand experience with witch doctors, the ancient animist rights of the traditional cultures over there, or a deep understanding of anthropology. He did, however know that there was no way this guy's name was *Larry*.

Larry handed Alan's credentials back to him with a disappointed grimace. He didn't like Alan. He didn't seem to like John very much, either.

They passed the checkpoint and continued through the building. A sweet smell wafted through the halls, gentle and light like a whiff of perfume.

"Sage," John said, noticing Alan sniffing the air. "They burn sage in here twice a day. It clears the air in the building, cleanses it."

"I suppose that will keep the evil hexes away" Alan said.

"Exactly." John said.

"That was the strangest security check I've gone through," Alan said.

"What, you mean Larry?" John asked.

"There is no way his name is Larry," Alan said.

"It is. Lawrence Umbutu. He's a shaman, like his father and grandfather were. Their family came over here as refugees when Larry was a kid. I don't know all the details, but it was something about a cow that wouldn't give milk," John said.

Alan thought about laughing, but the look on John's face wasn't cheerful. There was a dread in his eyes. He'd seen things like this before, and Alan could tell that it was the worst type of fear, probably one that he'd faced his whole life.

"Also," Alan said, "no metal detector? In a government building?"

"Alan, this is a town populated almost entirely with witches who can cause tornados, occultists that can summon demons, and, as you just met, shamans who can make the spirits of dead warriors destroy the food supply of entire nations. The last thing they're worried about is someone going nuts and shooting up the place," John said.

There was a stress in his voice. It was hard to tell if it was from their upcoming meeting with the Council, or just the things he dealt with daily as a cop in this town, but it was there. A sharpness in his tone. Alan got the feeling that if John wanted to, he could give his words fangs.

They stopped outside a wooden door. A uniformed guard stood outside, his hands folded over his belt.

"Detective John Weatherby and Detective Alan Schriever to see the Council," John said.

The stress was gone from his voice. He sounded stern, determined. It was a military tone, as though he was speaking to a subordinate.

The guard nodded and went through the door, closing it behind him. The two detectives stood in silence as they waited. Alan didn't actually know what they were waiting for.

A moment later the guard returned. He nodded at John and held the door open. John led the way through the door into a small vestibule where they faced another door.

"This is the Silence Room," John said. "It's part of the soundproofing for the Council Room."

A second later, a light came on over the door in front of them. John opened the door and the two detectives walked into the Council Room.

The room was covered in wood paneling. It was stained dark, with a high gloss finish that made the light glint off the details and carved surfaces. Unlike the artwork in the rest of the building, this room didn't have any depictions of scenes from mythology, just complex geometric patterns like the trim in a Victorian house. Ten raised desks stood in a semicircle around the room. At each desk sat a woman. They varied in age from late thirties to ancient, with a few having passed through ancient decades ago. Since they were all seated when he came in, Alan couldn't see how any of them got into the room, but his best guess was floating through the walls like Jacob Marley on a courtesy call.

"Detective Weatherby. Nice to see you again," one of the ancients who looked remarkably like a crow spoke up. There was a general *harrumph* of agreement from the gathered crones.

What was a group of witches called? A cornucopia? A gaggle?

"I see you've brought a friend," the same woman spoke again.

"Yes. This is Detective Alan Schriever of the Vienna Police. He is aiding me in investigating Aaron Burroughs' death," John gestured to Alan.

Alan stepped forward and waved.

"I am Tara Spencer, the head of this Council, Detective Schriever. I cannot express to you how sorry we are that the problems of our little town have spread to your city. Detective Weatherby," she said, turning to look at John, "it is very uncommon to bring an outsider into this town, and unheard of to bring one before this Council. Do you realize the possible impact of what you've done today?" she said.

Her lips were thin and drawn, her eyes hard.

"I do, Madame Spencer. However, outside aid has been called on before, and Detective Schriever is particularly well suited to work with me on this case. All we need is access to Aaron Burroughs' papers, which you've had moved to the Archive," John said, holding her stare.

"Detective Schriever," a much younger woman sitting at the far right end of the semicircle spoke up, "my name is Adrienne Cooper. Since you're in this chamber, I can only assume that Detective Weatherby has informed you as to what makes this county different than most places?"

Alan nodded.

"And what do you think about what you know?" she asked. Her tone had an edge to it. Alan had heard it from politicians before. She was working toward a point, and it wasn't a good one.

"I know I saw a man in Vienna jump to the roof of a two-story building from the ground. I know I saw a house today that for no particular reason has a second floor when it shouldn't. Beyond that, I don't have any proof that any of this is real," Alan said. He turned to face her, ready for the inevitable showdown.

"Proof?" she asked, standing. "You want proof?"

She put her arm out in front of her with her palm up, looking at John. As she raised her hand, Alan heard John groan behind him. He turned and saw John's face drawn with pain as his feet came off the ground.

Alan reacted. He reached to his side and drew his weapon, leveling it at Cooper.

"Let him go!" Alan commanded. The woman continued to lift her hand, raising John further from the floor.

Alan heard noises from the rest of the Council. He kept his eyes and his gun trained on Cooper.

"I said let him go, now!" he yelled.

"Ms. Cooper, put him down!" Madame Spencer said. She had stood up from her chair, a feat Alan didn't think she was capable of.

"Is this proof enough for you? Do you see my power?" Cooper screeched.

"I think that my coworkers might be robots, yesterday I saw a guy jump twenty feet straight up, my partner may or may not be a vampire, and my coffee maker hates me. You're not even the strangest thing I've seen today, and I *will* shoot you, lady." Alan said.

John was several feet off the ground now. His back arched awkwardly as his arms dangled at his sides.

"Adrienne Cooper, put him down *now!*" Madame Spencer yelled. Her words echoed through the room like high pitched thunder, blocking out any other noise.

Cooper looked at the rest of the Council, prompting Alan to do the same. The old women who just moments ago looked close to death were all standing, their advanced years seeming to have fallen away. Their eyes glinted in the light, their long silver hair flowing with the vigor of youth as they stepped forward, ready to take action.

Adrienne Cooper's hand lowered, then finally dropped. John fell to the floor with a thud. Alan leaned down to him.

"You alright?" Alan asked.

"Yeah," John said, "I'm fine." Alan helped him to his feet.

"Listen," Alan said, turning to Madame Spencer, "I know you need to keep your secret, and I know that I'm an outsider here, but me knowing about it isn't a threat to you."

"Explain, Detective." Madame Spencer said.

Alan took a deep breath. If he told them, it might be over right now. If he didn't, this case would definitely be over, at least for him.

"I just came back from a suspension. I had a nervous breakdown and spent six months in a mental institution. I've been off the job for a year. I'm pretty sure they brought me back in the hope that I'd screw up bad enough that they could finally fire me. Even if I did tell anyone, who would believe me?" he said.

Madame Spencer looked at him. It wasn't a stare. It was more like she was trying to read something in him, see if she could figure out what was behind his eyes.

"Detective Weatherby," she said after several moments of silence, "due to the unique nature of these events, and your partner's unusual situation and understanding, you will be allowed access to the Archive as you need it."

Adrienne Cooper interrupted her.

"You're going to give this blackblood and his lunatic partner access to all of this town's secrets?" she yelled.

The room got even quieter. All eyes were again on John.

"Miss Cooper," John finally said, "as you well know, I don't appreciate that term, and ask you to refrain from saying it again."

Alan watched him. He saw flashes of the night before, when Springheel Jack had commented on his mother. Flashes of something animal. It may have been the lighting.

"However," Madame Spencer said, "I caution you to use your better judgment in your investigation, and the archivist will accompany you."

"Of course," John said. "Thank you, Madame Spencer. Thank you, council members." He shot a look at Adrienne Cooper that could peel paint and turned to leave.

Alan nodded to Madame Spencer and followed John out of the room.

CHAPTER 8

Once outside the Town Hall, John pointed out the Archive.

"It's just around the corner," he said, walking in the direction of the building.

"Want to tell me what happened in there?" Alan said.

"I got assaulted, then I got insulted." John responded, still walking.

"Stop." Alan said.

John turned to face him. "What?"

"She called you a blackblood. What does that mean?" Alan asked.

John's shoulders softened. He fiddled with his hands for a moment.

"You remember me telling you about sins of the father following the son?" he asked.

"Yeah. That was right before you almost ate Springheel Jack." Alan said.

"Well, there are two types of power in our world. Light and dark. Creative and destructive. This doesn't mean good or evil, but dark powers are looked down upon." John said.

"Is that the side you come from?" Alan asked.

"It's the side my mom comes from. It shouldn't be an insult, but it's used to excuse prejudice," John said.

"How bad could she have been? Who was your mom?" Alan asked.

"Her name was Marguerite Harker, and she was a wonderful mother," John said.

Alan got the feeling that John meant that to end the conversation. He looked up at the sky, for the first time today noticing the fluffy white clouds that dotted the blue. It looked like cotton balls floating in... well... a blue sky.

"Why me?" Alan asked.

"What?" John asked.

"Why did you pick me? The Captain said that I was back against his wishes. That means someone requested my assignment to this case. Since you're the only cop who doesn't seem to think I'm nuts, I have to assume it was you," Alan said.

"You're right," John said. "I did request you for this case. When one of ours dies, we hear about it almost immediately. It's a safety precaution. But even before that, I knew about you. I know you were institutionalized, and I know that you're not actually delusional."

Alan looked at him, his eyes narrowed.

John continued. "You're not delusional. You find the shortest distance between two points, no matter how illogical it is. You accept even the most improbable things as potential answers. In normal life, that's the sort of thing that gets you labeled as a lunatic. But out here," John gestured to the town around them, "it's the kind of thing that lets you accept what you see."

"So you don't think I'm crazy?" Alan said, trying to keep his voice from cracking.

"No, you're crazy. Don't misunderstand me," John said. "But back there, in the Council room, you didn't stop to question if what you were seeing was real or not, or how it was being done. That's what a normal cop would do. You accepted and reacted to the situation as it was. That is what I need in a partner, because waiting for someone to figure out what's going on could get someone killed." John stopped for a second. He was looking at Alan with the same expression Tara Spencer had just a few minutes earlier. "You're crazy, but you're a good cop, a good detective, and you're the right kind of crazy," he said.

Alan watched him for a minute. John's eyes were hidden by his dark Wayfarers, his mouth set in a humorless line. He wasn't being nice, he wasn't being funny. He was stating this as a fact, like he was listing off a grocery list. It was as simple as that: According to John, Alan was simply the right guy for the job. But there was still something that bothered him more than anything else. More than John's strange background, this strange town, or anything he'd just seen or heard.

"One question," Alan said.

"Sure," John responded.

Alan studied him, looking John over.

"Does your hair *ever* move? I mean, seriously. It's kinda breezy out here, and there's nothing, not a single errant hair, nothing out of place," Alan said.

John's brow furrowed again. His mouth moved as though there were too many words to say and yet no words that could convey the feeling.

"I... Yes, my hair moves. It... I mean... That's your... Dear God I... Okay," John put his hands on his hips and stared at the ground. His foot tapped out a frustrated rhythm. "I like to look clean and neat, that's all. Let's go to the Archive," John turned and continued up the street, with Alan close behind.

The outside of the Archive looked like it had been designed by a prison architect in the nineteen seventies. It had tall, narrow, inescapable windows and a single solid steel door in the front. The façade was concrete, not blocks or anything decorative; just hard, smooth, unnecessarily imposing concrete in dark grey. From the outside it was clear that you could learn nothing but how to be harder, meaner, and more dangerous in a place like that. It looked just like Alan's high school.

"It never ceases to amaze me. If you make a place look like somewhere people don't want to be, people won't go there," John said. He opened up the door and walked into the world's smallest supermax prison.

Alan followed him in. On the inside, it looked a bit like an old study, or some crazy professor's home office: There were books and papers stacked all over the room, wooden shelves lined every available inch of wall space. There was a small metal desk and chair set back in the corner, facing the door. On the far wall there was another solid metal door.

"Can I help you?" a small, wavering voice said. It was coming from a stairwell set into the side wall behind the desk. Alan hadn't noticed it before, or maybe it hadn't been there at all. At this point, the walls could be dripping blood, and Alan didn't think he'd care much.

"Doctor, It's John Weatherby. Detective Weatherby," John said, walking forward and yelling up the stairs.

"Oh, my goodness John!" the voice said. Hurried footsteps echoed in the hallway beyond the stairs.

Moments later, a man whose form perfectly fit the voice that came from it appeared. He looked even older than Mrs. Morlin, and twice as crazy.

"John Weatherby. As I live. I haven't seen you since, when was it?" the old man asked.

"College. Right after I got back," John said, smiling.

It was the first time Alan had really seen him smile. It was a warm, natural smile. It belonged in a men's clothing catalogue. The kind that show women how they should dress their boyfriends.

"How are you, Doctor?" John asked, still smiling.

"I have been well, been well. The old hip has been acting up, and of course, I lost Tamara this year..." the old doctor trailed off.

"I'm sorry to hear that, Doctor. I know you loved her," John said.

"Oh, don't," The old man said, smiling. "Death comes for all of us eventually. But I see you've brought a friend?" he asked.

"Yes," John said, motioning to Alan to step forward. "Doctor Federico Alighieri, this is my partner, Detective Alan Schriever."

Alan extended his hand. "It's very nice to meet you, Doctor Alighieri. I'm sorry to hear about your wife," Alan said.

John and Dr. Alighieri both looked at him. It was a confused look, but more of a pitiful one than he normally got. Now he was confused, too, and he didn't know why.

"My wife, you say?" Doctor Alighieri asked.

"Yes, Tamara. You just mentioned that you'd lost her this year?" Alan asked.

"Oh, no. Tamara wasn't my wife, dear boy. But she was a faithful companion," the Doctor said, smiling at John, who was smiling back.

Alan felt once again like he'd missed the joke.

"His *car*, Alan," John said, taking mercy on him.

"A nineteen fifty-five Cadillac Coupe Deville. Bought her new," the Doctor said, a poetic spring in his words.

"What finally killed her?" John asked.

"Oh, you know. The normal things: Age, bad breaks, an oak tree," the Doctor said, flopping down behind his desk. "So, what brings the country's most overeducated detective and his slightly confused partner to my little office today?" he asked.

"We're looking into the death of Aaron Burroughs," Alan said.

"Oh, I heard about that. Sad business. Did I hear right that he'd been turned into jam or preserves or something similar?" Alighieri asked.

"We can't really talk about an…" Alan started.

"Jelly, actually. No idea what caused it," John interrupted.

Alan pulled John back from the desk.

"Should we really be discussing this with him?" Alan whispered. "It's completely against protocol to discuss an ongoing investigation."

"Trust me; he's been keeping this town's secrets longer than anyone can remember. If he knows what happened to Burroughs, it's no secret. The reason he has this job is because he knows what to say and what to keep hidden," John said.

"Also, I have remarkably good hearing for a man of my vintage," Doctor Alighieri said.

Alan gave him a sheepish grin.

"I don't know what could have caused his death. I've heard of all sorts of rites and spells and incantations in my day, but nothing quite like that," he added.

"Actually, we're here to look through Aaron's papers. They've already been moved." John said. "We think they may hold the key to what happened."

"You think it might have something to do with his work, then? Or maybe Miss Jackson. I hope not on the latter. She is a lovely girl," Alighieri said.

"His work, mainly, but you never know what you might find, do you?" John said.

"No, no you don't," Alighieri said, a knowing smile on his wrinkled lips.

There was a moment where no one spoke. The Doctor's words hung in the air like a threat, like a rainbow, like a trout trapped between universes. Alan was crap at metaphors.

"Well, then! Best we get this show on the road. You boys have *investigating* to do!" Alighieri said, hopping out of his chair with an impressive vigor.

He pulled an old, leather bound book off the shelf and opened it to the inside cover.

"Come here, Mr. Schriever," he said.

Alan walked over to the desk and stood before the wizened old visage.

"Give me your hand," the old man said.

Alan stuck his hand out. Alighieri grabbed it and stabbed it with a needle. Alan yelped.

"Oh, you baby!" Alighieri said. "It's just a pin prick. Everyone in town gets one!"

He took Alan's bleeding finger and pressed it into a box drawn on the first page of the book. The blood pooled for a second and then seeped into the paper, disappearing.

"Now," the old man said, "write your name in the box."

Alan did as he was told. Seconds after he finished writing, the ink disappeared, too.

"What, exactly, just happened, Doctor?" he asked.

Alighieri smiled at him. "This is the Archive Ledger. Everyone who lives in town or has ever visited the Archive for any reason has their name and blood in here. It lets us keep the protection updated."

"Protection?" Alan asked.

"The Archive is protected by a multitude of spells, hexes, and other more modern deterrents. Your blood in that book lets the building know you're allowed to be here, and let's Doctor Alighieri know if you ever come back. This is the most secure building in Darke County," John said.

"So, what would happen if someone came in who wasn't allowed?" Alan asked.

"Oh, they'd die," Doctor Alighieri said, "now, let's get you into the stacks!"

The old doctor led the way through the door at the back of the room. It wasn't locked. The room beyond was lined with more shelves, identical to the ones in the ante room. They were labeled by last name in a beautiful script. Some had first names listed on specific shelves. He noticed that there were blocks of shelves dedicated to single families. With how long this place had been running, and all the old families who stayed here, there were hundreds of first names in some of the families.

Even though it looked like a prison from the outside, there wasn't much physical security. Alan figured that the fear of immediate death was probably enough of a deterrent, and kept others from trying when the first guy failed. He wondered how many people had failed.

"Two-hundred-thirty-five," Alighieri said.

"Apropos of nothing," Alan added. Damn. Out loud thought bubble.

"You wondered how many people had been killed in this building, didn't you?" Alighieri asked.

Alan stopped and stared at the little old man's glimmering eyes.

"Are you in my head? Do I need a tin foil helmet to talk to you?" Alan asked.

"Nothing of the sort, my boy. It was simple experience: You tell someone that a building can kill people, and the first thing they'll think, especially a homicide detective, is how many have died. I don't need to get into people's heads. Way too much sex in there for a man of my age," he said, poking Alan in the forehead. "Now, back here is the Burroughs Family," He pointed down another row of shelves toward a back corner.

"This place is too big," Alan said, looking around.

"Getting tired?" John asked.

"No, it's *too big*. The building isn't big enough to hold all this," Alan said.

"It's like Burroughs' house. Doctor Alighieri used a similar spell to make room for the new arrivals," John said.

Alan nodded. One thing he'd learned in the hospital: sometimes it was just better to smile and nod.

"This," Alighieri said pointing to a shelf, "is the collected work of the life of one Aaron Burroughs: Born in Darke County, Ohio, died in Vienna, Ohio. Are you going to use the study room, or just spread the papers out on the floor?"

Alan looked at John, who was looking at him.

"I think we'll use the study room if that's okay," Alan said, grabbing a box.

CHAPTER 9

Burroughs' entire personal papers consisted of three file boxes. This was just his research, personal planners, and correspondence from the last five years. None of it was in chronological order.

"They just pulled it off the shelves and stuffed it in boxes," John said. "We're lucky he didn't live longer, or we'd be here for months trying to figure this out."

They started separating the papers into personal, work, and research piles. It was quickly clear that he had more research than anything else.

Alan pulled a small scrap out of a box.

"A napkin. He kept a napkin," he said.

"What's on it?" John asked.

"Numbers, some kind of formula. It's covered back and front with math. Why wouldn't he transfer this to paper?" Alan said.

John shrugged. "I have no idea," he said. "Put it in the research stack."

They dug for hours. There were old books, pages photocopied from old books, entire notebooks filled with mathematical formulas and no explanations, nothing that made sense. The time went by, grinding like a car with no clutch. Alan's back hurt, his eyes hurt. His hands were covered in tiny paper cuts. He kept getting one of those intense itches on the bottom of his foot that wouldn't go away, the kind you get when you're driving that makes you pull over on the side of the highway. So he had to keep taking off his shoe to scratch it.

After what seemed like hours, John made a sound.

"What's this?" He was holding up a sheet of parchment. It looked even older than the Archive Register. Just a single sheet.

Alan leaned over the desk to get a better look. The sheet was covered in symbols, words in Latin and another language, and a mixture of math and letters that weren't in the alphabet.

"I don't know," Alan said, "but that doesn't look like anything else we've found. It's older, and I haven't seen those symbols in any of his notes."

"Doctor Alighieri!" John yelled.

The old man opened the door. He must have been sitting outside the whole time.

"Yes?" he said, coming up to the table.

"Do you recognize this? It doesn't fit with anything else we've found," John said.

Alighieri slipped on reading glasses and studied the paper.

"This is Latin," he said, pointing to a phrase, "and this is old Italian, Renaissance, if my memory serves."

"What does it say?" John asked.

"It's a formula, a chemical formula. It looks like something about minerals. What was it with?" he said.

"I found it in here, with a bunch of notes," John said, pointing to a manila folder on the table in front of him.

Alighieri picked up the folder and glanced through it. He read silently as he turned pages, nodding his head every few seconds. Finally, he set the folder back on the table.

"Well, that certainly explains why Mr. Burroughs returned to Darke County, doesn't it?" Alighieri said.

"What does?" Alan asked.

"What? Oh, I haven't said, have I? No, I haven't. It was Alchemy, my boy. A favorite subject of mine, actually. It seems that your physicist was using his extensive knowledge of science to try and finally crack the Alchemic code," Alighieri said.

"I thought this guy was a scientist. He was trying to turn lead into gold?" Alan asked.

"Oh, that's only one stage of the process, an early step in learning how to create something truly marvelous," Alighieri suddenly had just a touch of an Italian accent.

"The real goal of alchemy is a life elixir. The goal is to learn how to make a certain crystal, and from that, you can make a liquid that will keep you alive and young forever," John said.

"Oh for Christ's sake," Alan said. "Seriously? He was looking for something from a kid's book?"

"Don't underestimate the reality of the Philosopher's Stone, Detective," Alighieri said. "Also, I found those books quite entertaining. It seems from his notes that Mr. Burroughs was using a combination of science and magic. He was bombarding rare magical materials with charged particles while applying a spell to them, and he may have had some minor success."

"What makes you think that?" John asked.

"Right here," Alighieri pointed at a note on one of the papers, "it says *success*, couldn't be clearer."

"So he was succeeding somewhat. That doesn't explain why we found him as a human jelly mold in an alley," John said.

"No, but this might have something to do with it," Alan said. He was holding a yellow sticky note. "It says 'S, 8:30 Tues.' then gives an address. That's the night before he died. Could that be Sarah?"

John took the note and read it. "The handwriting looks like his, but I know this address. It's not anywhere you'd go on a date. It's an old derelict warehouse," he said. "I don't know why he'd be meeting Sarah there."

"We should check it out," Alan said.

"We should talk to Sarah first," John said, "she might be able to give us some insight."

"Then I'll leave you boys to it," Dr. Alighieri said. "Just leave things where they are, I have to get them organized and properly catalogued, anyway."

The three men walked out of the study room and into the Archive. Alighieri led them back through the rows of shelves toward the door.

As they neared the front, Alan noticed a huge book open on a plinth. It was nearly three feet across and looked older than the other books Alan had seen.

"Doctor, what is that?" he asked, pointing at the volume.

"Ahh!" Alighieri exclaimed. "That might be the most important book in the whole Archive, at least to some people."

He led Alan over to the book, which looked even bigger up close.

"This, my boy, is the collected ancestry of everyone in Darke County. From the first families to the newest arrivals. It records all of their comings and goings, births and deaths, and major hereditary abilities," Alighieri said.

"Some of the people here inherit their magic? I was under the impression it was something that you learned," Alan said.

"Some people learn magic the hard way, through study and practice. Others, the old families especially, are born with a natural talent for one type of magic or another," the doctor said. "You see, the old families were like nobility. They all were naturals, and they thought that no one who wasn't should learn magic. Of course this changed over the years."

"For most of them," John interjected.

"Yes, quite right," Alighieri said. "In the past two centuries, the bloodlines have thinned, people with different natural abilities have come in, some not even magical, just *different*. Some of them are partially supernatural, some of them fully, and some of them are simply brilliant thinkers the world has turned its back on. They've all come here, and they're recorded in this lineage. Every family has a history, and this book tracks all of it, whether the family member is in Darke County or not."

"Interesting," Alan said. "So will I end up in this book?"

"You, probably not. There are strict rules as to who gets their lineage in the book. But take no shame in that, Detective. You're a man of the modern times, a better, egalitarian time when a man is judged simply on his own sins, and not those of his ancestors. It is a subject I'm far too familiar with," Alighieri looked for a moment sad, then his face brightened again.

He led them out into the front room. The men shook hands.

"If you want to be in the book, I could make that happen," Alighieri told Alan.

"I thought you said there were rules," Alan said, shaking his hand.

"Rules? I am Alighieri!" he said, a wide grin spreading across his wrinkled face as he spread his arms wide.

"It was nice to meet you, Doctor," Alan said.

"You too, my boy. You too. Good luck to you in finding the root of your mystery," Alighieri said, walking back up the stairs behind the desk.

CHAPTER 10

As the two men stepped onto the street, the sun was just dipping behind the buildings. Alan stared at the brilliant colors; reds and oranges and yellows and purples in layers like poorly mixed sherbet. Or a sunset, it could be like a sunset.

"The most overeducated detective in the state, huh?" he asked.

"I went to college, just like you," John said.

"Why does that sound like an understatement?" Alan said.

"This is why I like you. Nothing gets by, does it?" John asked.

"Still not an answer," Alan said.

"Okay. It sounds like an understatement because it is," John said.

"I went to Ohio State. Where did you go?" Alan asked.

"Cambridge." John said.

"Cambridge. So a Harvard man." Alan said.

"No, Cambridge, England. I was a student of Peterhouse, Cambridge," John said.

"That makes you well educated. Alighieri said you were *over* educated. That can't be all of it," Alan said.

"Okay," John said.

He was staring at the sunset. Alan couldn't help thinking that John saw more in it than he did.

"Undergrad at Cambridge, Masters at Harvard, Doctorate at Oxford. You happy now?" John said.

"What subject?" Alan asked.

"History. That's enough," John said.

"One more thing," Alan said.

John shot him a look.

"What is Doctor Alighieri's degree in?" Alan asked.

"Theology. He's Doctor of Theology," John said. "Can we get to the car now? We've got a potential witness to interview."

John started up the sidewalk. People were out on the street now; the town square was alive with bodies. People were chatting and enjoying the cool evening breeze as it blew through the trees.

Alan watched as they went by. Every single one of them was different. Different from each other, yes, but even more different from anyone outside this little county. He'd been wondering why they would need such secrecy to protect themselves. Why would the world care anymore what they were capable of? Did it really matter if all the stuff people thought were just myth and superstition was real? He saw Larry, the guard from the Town Hall, walking up the other side of the street with his lunch pail. He met a pretty woman, probably in her mid-forties. The two embraced. Then Alan thought about why Larry was even here: Where he grew up, he could have been stoned to death for what he was. Alan had seen it on the news not long ago. Not what he did, not what he looked like, the simple random chance that he'd been born into that particular family.

It made him think about John. He didn't know what secret John's mother had that John was so careful in protecting, but it was bad enough that even here there was a prejudice against it. If she'd really been a vampire, or whatever the real world equivalent is, then her life could have been spent on the run, chased from town to town as her secret was discovered. She would have been a criminal just because of who she was, just like Larry.

It started to make sense as he watched John getting in the SUV a block away.

"Excuse me?" a tiny little voice said from somewhere closer to the ground.

Alan looked down. There was a little blonde girl, maybe ten years old, standing in front of him.

"Yes? How can I help you?" Alan said. He was never very good with kids, but he did his best.

"My name is Tracy. What's yours?" she said.

"My name is Alan. How can I help you, Tracy?" Alan said.

"You seem like a nice man. I want to give you a flower," Tracy said.

"Okay, Tracy. Where are your parents?" Alan asked.

"Oh, my mom is right over there," Tracy said, pointing to a stunning woman standing across the street in the square. The woman waved at Alan.

"Okay. I'll take a flower, Tracy," Alan said.

Tracy reached out to hand him the flower. There was a squeal of tires next to them as John's SUV stopped, followed by the slamming of a door. John came running around the front of the SUV.

"Tracy!" he yelled. "What have I told you?"

The little girl scowled at John and pulled back the flower.

"And what have I told your mother?" John said, glaring across the street.

Tracy gave John a stare and walked back across the street to her mother. The two of them continued to look at John with eyes that could bore through rock.

"That was close," John said.

"Yes, it was," Alan responded. "Why did you just yell at a little girl for giving me a flower?" he asked.

John took a deep breath. "That little girl," he said, "is a succubus. So is her mother."

Alan tried to make his expression not blank, but couldn't decide what to put there.

"A succubus. Female demon that seduces its prey. At least that's what the stories say," John said.

"So, that ten year old girl was going to seduce me?" Alan asked. "I don't think it would have worked."

"Not today. If you accept a gift from a succubus, you're marked as theirs. They start collecting when they're children, and when they become of age, they start calling their men in. You wouldn't be able to resist it, either. The minute they want you, you'll go, no questions asked. Then they drain the life out of you over a period of years. When you're dead, they call the next man," John said.

"So what you're telling me is, they're women?" Alan said.

"In the worst possible way," John said, walking back around the SUV.

Alan got in the passenger side.

Once they were situated, John glanced at Alan.

"Listen," he said, "this is all new to you, and you know now why I chose you for this. But there are things you don't understand about this town and the people in it, so there's going to be a learning curve."

Alan nodded.

"So for now," John looked at Alan and smiled, "don't take gifts from children."

John pulled away from the curb.

CHAPTER 11

A little while later, they were standing in Sarah Jackson's front room. It was a small suburban house, like every other one on the street, but the longer they were there, the tenser John got.

"I met Aaron about a year ago," Sarah said. "We were both in line at Drucilla's, and we just hit it off."

"Let me guess, an octopus lady who grants wishes to mermaids?" Alan asked.

John was pacing the room, looking at things on shelves while they spoke.

"No, Drucilla's Coffee, just off Main. He asked me if I'd tried the Pumpkin latte. I told him it was good, then he confessed that he didn't drink coffee, he'd only asked to have a reason to talk to me," Sarah said. She managed a smile and a small laugh, but it was forced.

She was a pretty girl, in her late twenties. Her hair was long, almost to her waist, and extremely curly. Her soft, round face held hazel eyes. They were wet with tears, and the lids were pink, worn raw from wiping them away. She definitely wasn't a robot. She was a witch, and that somehow didn't make Alan feel any better.

"Did you know what he was working on?" Alan asked.

"Yes, I knew he was trying to create the Philosopher's Stone. It was the whole reason he'd come back to town. He knew there was no way he'd be allowed to do that kind of research on a college campus without being laughed out of his job, so he came back here, where it was safe," her voice trailed off a bit.

"Did you ever see him working? Did you notice anything unusual about his method?" Alan asked.

"I'm not a physicist, Detective Schriever. But on the magic side of it, it all made sense. His spells were as safe as they could be, and he was working in a controlled environment, shielded from outside forces. But he never let me be there when he was running his actual experiments; he said the high energy particles were dangerous, that they put off a lot of radiation," she said.

"What about these rare materials he was working with? Do you know if any of those were dangerous?" John said.

"No, not that I know of. Most of them are pretty common in our world. Used for building apparatus and cleansing and blessing ceremonies. Of course, anything used the wrong way can be dangerous," she said.

"Aaron wasn't a witch, how did he get these materials? Did you supply them?" Alan asked.

"Do you know much about magic, Detective?" Sarah asked.

"I'm learning," Alan said.

"Well, there are different types of magic users. Some are capable of physical feats directly, like what you'd call telekinesis. Some can manipulate nature. They're the ones who can make it rain or snow or drought. Others are skilled in creating potions and things of that nature," she said.

"And what about you?" Alan asked.

"I am a blood witch. Sanguimancer is the proper term. I use my blood to power spells and effect things magically," she said.

"They're rare," John said. "It's a trait found only among the old families and no one else."

"Yes, that's true," Sarah said.

"So if he didn't get these materials from you, who would he have gotten them from?" Alan asked.

"I don't understand how this will help," Sarah said.

"We're just trying to understand everything we can about his life. Any detail might lead us to an answer," John said turning to face Sarah for the first time since they'd started talking.

"He could get them from anywhere, there are tons of sources. This stuff isn't regulated," Sarah said.

"Did you see Aaron Tuesday night?" John asked.

"Tuesday? No. I was visiting with my mother Tuesday. I taught my last dance class and went straight to her house. Why do you ask?" Sarah said.

"We have evidence that he was meeting with someone the night he died, the note just said 'S'. We were hoping you could shed some light on it," Alan said.

"No, I don't know who he was going to meet. He was having trouble finding Clarisium, though," Sarah said.

"Clarisium?" John asked.

"Yeah. It's a rare material. Seriously rare, and with really unusual properties. He thought it might be the key to finally creating the stone," Sarah said.

"Does anyone make Clarisium that you know of? Anyone in town?" Alan asked.

"No, it's almost impossible to make, and almost as hard to find. It takes years to complete the combination of potions and spells to get a finished product, and even then it usually fails. You can't even buy it; you have to convince someone to give it to you. That's one of the weird properties. If you buy it, it will turn to ash in your hands," Sarah said.

"And he was looking for some for his experiment?" John asked.

"Yes. He was complaining that he couldn't find anyone who had any at all. There might be a few small pieces, but the people who have it never tell anyone unless they want to get rid of it, so it's impossible to know for sure if there's any at all," Sarah said.

Alan looked at John. It was time to go.

"Okay, Miss Jackson," Alan said, standing up. "We'll let you know if we need anything else."

Sarah turned to John. "Please, find out what happened? Aaron was a good man. He was good to me."

"I'll do my job," John said. He walked out of the house.

"It was nice to meet you, Sarah. I'm sorry for your loss," Alan said. He shook her hand and followed John.

CHAPTER 12

Twenty minutes later, the two detectives were sitting in the parked SUV outside an abandoned building in an industrial-looking section of Arcanum.

"I didn't know Arcanum had a section of town like this," Alan said, looking out the window.

"It shouldn't," John said. "These buildings were part of the Project Rainbow base. They should have been torn down years ago, but the Council keeps swearing they're going to come up with a plan to revitalize this district. They've been saying the same thing since the fifties."

"Huh. I guess small town bureaucracy is the same no matter what town you're in. It doesn't really matter if it's being run by witches, robots, or any other kind of conspiracy." Alan mused.

"That's strangely the sanest thing you've said all day," John said

"What are we looking for here?" Alan asked.

"I have no idea. This was the address Burroughs wrote down, so if he was coming here to try and get to one of the parties, there's got to be evidence of it. People don't come here often," John said.

"Makes sense. I'm sure there's all sorts of crazy curses and bad energy hanging around a place like this," Alan said.

John looked over at Alan. He stared for a moment, cocking his head to the side before turning away and opening the door.

"No, it's really, really creepy," he said, hopping out of the SUV.

Alan caught up with him in a few steps. The building *was* creepy, even creepier as they got close. It was huge, taking up half of a long city block. The windows were set high in the walls, well out of reach of anyone without a ladder, or Springheel Jack. The whole structure was made of cinder blocks. It looked every bit like the kind of place you should never wander into uninvited, and if you were invited, to seriously consider who was inviting you before you decided to show up. He'd seen body dumps that looked more hospitable.

John looked over the steel door.

"This hasn't been opened in years," he said, examining the frame and testing the padlock.

"The dirt hasn't even been disturbed," Alan said, pointing to the ground.

"Well, if they went in, they didn't use this door. Time to walk the perimeter," John said.

Alan pulled his flashlight out of his pocket and turned it on. After so long on suspension, he was surprised he'd remembered it. Old habits die hard. Then he noticed that John wasn't using a flashlight, though there wasn't a streetlight for blocks in any direction, and it was a cloudy night.

"Forget your flashlight?" Alan asked.

"No, I can see fine," John said.

Alan couldn't see John's eyes, he could only imagine that they were shimmering in the dim light just like they had been last night when they were looking for Jack.

They walked around the huge building, inspecting the ground for any sign that someone had been there. There were footprints, but that didn't mean anything. This place was in town, people came by occasionally to check on the place, others just walked by. Also, there was no town in America that didn't have a few places teenagers thought that their parents didn't know about.

They were on the last side of the building when John stopped near the wall.

"Do you smell that?" he asked.

"I smell lots of things. Which one do you mean?" Alan asked.

"Bleach," John said.

Alan walked up next to John and focused. He could smell it, a whiff of bleach in the air, hanging around the wall of the building. John stepped up to the wall and inhaled sharply.

"And blood," he said.

Once again, Alan followed John's lead. Stepping up to the wall, he inhaled through his nose. He smelled wall. And bleach, but mostly wall.

"Wait here." John said. He took off around the corner toward the SUV. Moments later he was back with a flashlight and a squirt bottle.

"You're going to clean it and get a better look?" Alan asked.

"It's Luminal and a blacklight," John said.

Alan stepped back from the wall. John turned on the blacklight and started spraying the wall with the Luminal. Wherever he shined the light, Alan could see glowing lines appear. There were two large, concentric circles. The space between them was filled with what looked like squiggles.

"Okay, I know I ask a lot of questions, but this one is kind of important: What in the hell is *that?*"

"It's a portal. A blood magic gateway. This is why Burroughs came here. This is how they've been getting to the parties. They've been using magic to travel in and out of Darke County right under my nose," John said.

He sounded pissed. Somehow Alan thought this was more personal than just a mysterious death.

"I thought blood magic was okay, that it was one of the normal things that happened around here," Alan said.

"Oh, it is. Around *here*. But the use of magic outside of Darke County is strictly forbidden by both the law and the Social Club rules. They're using it to travel out so that no one sees them leaving. There's a Sanguimancer doing this," John said.

Alan thought about Sarah, John's strange reaction seeing the picture in Burroughs' house, how quiet he was when they'd interviewed her. It *was* personal, more than he was saying.

"It's going to take weeks to get DNA from this," John said.

"The bleach might make it..." Alan said. He'd stopped mid-sentence. His brain was reaching for something. It was just beyond him. There was something he'd seen. Something he'd seen today.

Something that had something to do with blood. Not Sarah. Something else. Something about...

"Get a sample," Alan said. "We don't need DNA."

John pulled a small tube with a Q-Tip in it out of his pocket and rubbed it on the bloodstain, closing the Q-Tip in the tube when he was done.

"We need to go back to the Archive," Alan said.

The detectives rushed back to the SUV and sped across town.

A few minutes later they arrived in front of the Archive. John had crossed the town in half the time it had taken to get out to the abandoned building in the first place. Alan jumped out of the SUV.

"Is he still here?" Alan asked.

"He lives here. Running the Archive is a full time job. He's always on call. Witches don't keep normal business hours," John said, rapping on the door.

A few minutes later, Alighieri opened the door.

"Yes?" he said, blinking behind his spectacles. "What's the commotion?"

"I have no idea," John said, "but my partner seemed to think we needed to hurry over here. Why were we in such a hurry, Alan?"

"Umm… because we're trying to solve a mystery, and every moment counts?" Alan said. "I don't know. A sense of urgency seemed appropriate at the time."

"Well, what can I do to help you solve your mystery, Detective Schriever?" Alighieri said, an amused tone sneaking into his question.

Alan and John walked into the front office of the Archive.

"Doctor, that book I gave a blood sample to earlier. Could you get it out for me? I'd like to try something," Alan said.

Doctor Alighieri pulled the leather bound tome down from the shelf and set it on the desk.

"John, the Q-Tip?" Alan asked.

John reached into his jacket pocket and pulled out the blood sample. He handed it to Alan.

"What are you going to try?" John said.

Alan turned to Dr. Alighieri, "Doctor, you said this book has a blood sample of everyone in town?"

"Well, yes," Dr. Alighieri said, "everyone who is of age to enter the Archive."

"How old do you have to be to enter?" Alan asked.

"Sixteen," John said. "What are you getting at?"

"Okay, so we have a book that has everyone's blood samples, like a biometric scanner. Or an RFID chip. You input it once and then it's stored and records whenever that person comes by," Alan said.

"Yes, that's pretty much exactly how it works. But I don't see what you're trying to say," Dr. Alighieri said.

Alan sighed. "I really can't believe that two people with doctorates who live in a town full of magicians don't understand this."

"The half completed thoughts of a mental patient? I will admit that the inner workings of your mind are something that neither my unusual upbringing nor my immense and incredibly expensive education have prepared me to foretell," John said.

"Oh for God's sake," Alan said, looking at Dr. Alighieri's blank face. He noticed that somehow Alighieri managed to express everything John had just said by simply staring. Alan wondered if that was the same face he'd been making the past couple days. He needed to stop that. It looked dumb.

Alan opened the book to the first page. "It's a password, and if it functions in any way like every other password…" He uncovered the Q-Tip and rubbed it in the box that had previously held his blood.

"Holy crap," John said. "I can't believe I never thought of that."

"Neither can I," Alighieri mumbled.

Ink started to appear in the box. "Then it should tell us if a password has already been taken," Alan said.

The three men gathered around, staring at the page.

"It's faint," John said.

"The sample isn't pure. Rub it again," Alighieri said.

Alan reapplied the sample.

"There. Now it's better. I can't read the handwriting, though. What does that say?" Alan said.

"The first letter of the first name is an S," John said.

"That makes sense, it fits the note we found." Alan said.

Alighieri pulled a magnifying glass out of a desk drawer.

"The first letter of the last name looks like another S," he said. "No, wait. It's not an S. It's a loopy J. I think the second letter of the first name…"

"Is an A," John said. "The name is Sarah Jackson."

"What does Sarah have to do with your mystery?" Alighieri asked.

"Doctor," Alan said, "this sample came from an illegal magic portal that people are using to travel to meetings or parties of some kind in Vienna."

"I can't believe Sarah would be mixed up in something like that." Alighieri said.

John stared at the wall. "I can," he said. "Alan, let's go."

John walked out the door without waiting for Alan. As they got in the SUV, John was angry, but a different kind of angry than before. He seemed more like a pissed-off older brother than a bloodthirsty killer.

"You're not telling me something," Alan said.

"You're very observant," John said, slamming the truck into gear and screeching away from the curb.

CHAPTER 13

They drove to Sarah's house in silence. Alan could feel the SUV accelerate and then decelerate over and over, as John was trying to stay under the speed limit. He knew the feeling. All John wanted to do right now was turn on the lights and sirens and gun the engine. He wanted to be there *yesterday*.

All the same, they arrived. John pulled the car into the driveway. Last time they had parked on the street, but parking in the driveway blocked Sarah's car. It was a normal procedure when you thought you'd be arresting someone to block their vehicle in.

The walked to the door. Before knocking, John turned to Alan.

"Let me handle this," John said.

"You sure you're good for it?" Alan asked.

"Yeah. I'm fine. This is my job. I'm just arresting a suspect," John said, knocking on the door.

A few seconds passed and Sarah answered.

"What the hell did you think you were doing?" John screamed, pushing his way past her.

"John, what the hell? What are you talking about?" Sarah said.

"Sit down. Sit down right now," John commanded.

Sarah did as she was told, dropping into a chair in the front room.

"John, what's going on?" She asked.

"I gave you a chance, Sarah. Ten years ago. You said you'd go straight, and you lied to me!" John screamed again.

"John," Alan said, "calm down."

"No," John responded. His voice was a little lower than a scream, but had no less menace.

"John, I really don't know what you're talking about. Tell me what happened," Sarah said.

"We found your blood, Sarah. On the portal Aaron went through. It was your blood. It was you. You lied about the whole thing," John said.

"I didn't, John, I swear," Sarah said. "I made you that promise and I kept it. I haven't done anything wrong in ten years!" she was close to sobbing now, her face in her hands.

"Are you cold?" Alan asked, interrupting.

"No, why?" Sarah said.

John looked at Alan there was a mixture of anger and confusion in his eyes. It was a look Alan was used to.

"It's a pretty warm night. You don't have the air conditioning on," Alan said.

"No, I don't. I don't like to waste electricity," Sarah said.

"Do you donate blood, Ms. Jackson?" Alan asked.

"What? No. I wouldn't dare," Sarah said.

"It's against the rules for sanguimancers to donate blood," John said.

"You're wearing long sleeves, Ms. Jackson," Alan said. "Show me your arms."

Sarah folded her arms over her chest. "I won't. I don't have to," she said.

"Sarah, pull up your sleeves, or I'll do it for you, in front of the Council," John said.

"I took every precaution," Sarah said, pulling up her sleeve. "I even drove all the way to Vienna so that no one would know that my blood was special."

She had a small puncture wound inside her right elbow.

"Jesus, Sarah. Do you know what kind of trouble you could get in for that?" John said.

"Worse than having your barge into my house and accuse me?" Sarah asked.

"Much worse. Donating Sanguimancer blood is considered practicing dark magic," John said.

"You wouldn't," Sarah said.

"I'm sorry, what?" Alan asked.

"Alan, the Council makes the laws for all the people in Darke County. They make specific rules and punishments based on the specific group you're from. Witches, occultists, scientists, ect. They stick very much to the old *let the punishment fit the crime* attitude," John said.

"So for a witch's crime, a witch's punishment," Alan said.

"Yes," Sarah said, "and the punishment for practicing black magic is immolation."

"Burning?" Alan asked. "They'll burn you at the stake?"

"Yes. A witch's punishment for a witch's crime," John said.

"I'm not totally okay with that," Alan said. "Seems a bit harsh for donating blood."

"It is. The same as stealing a Sanguimancer's blood or hiding activities from the Council," John said.

"So whoever's throwing the parties faces the same thing, then. Sounds like a pretty good reason to frame someone," Alan said.

"It is," John said. "Sarah, you said you drove all the way to Vienna to donate. Did you recognize anyone there?"

"No. If I had, I wouldn't have done it," she said.

"And how long have you been donating blood?" John asked.

"Every couple of months for the past year or so," Sarah said.

"So there's a chance someone would have figured out where you were going. Hold on, I have to make a call." John pulled his phone from his pocket and walked out of the room.

Alan could hear him through the thin walls, but couldn't understand what he was saying. Even so, his tone was intimidating.

"Do you know who he is?" Sarah asked.

"Who, John?" Alan asked.

"Yes. Your new partner. Do you know who he *really* is?" she asked.

"To be honest, no. I do know that he's not a robot, not a witch, and not the person who made my coffee maker hate me," Alan said.

"That makes no sense at all," Sarah said. "John Weatherby is the kind of man who can take a life or save one with the same amount of passion. He's saved more than he's killed, but don't kid yourself into thinking he's not dangerous."

"Also, he's possibly part vampire or something, can apparently run really fast, and can intimidate hardened police captains. Sounds like my kind of partner," Alan said.

"You're crazy." Sarah said.

"I know, and so does he." Alan said.

He looked her over as they waited for John to come back. She was pretty, he'd noticed that before. But beyond that there was strength in her eyes, defiance. When John was accusing her, she seemed strangely loyal. If it had been him on the other end of that, Alan couldn't have stood up. She did, but it wasn't about self-preservation. He could see that now. She didn't want John to think badly of her. She cared about him enough to lie to him. Alan could see why John liked her.

"Okay, good," John said. He slid his phone back into his pocket.

"Kyle Erikson. Do you recognize the name?" he asked Sarah.

"No, should I?" she said.

"He's a Sanguimancer. Worked at the donation center here until a few months ago, when he transferred to Vienna. What center did you use there?"

"If Sanguimancer blood is so dangerous, why would they even have a donation center here?" Alan asked.

"There are plenty of people here who want to help. Anyone who *isn't* a Sanguimancer can donate whenever they like, just like anyone else," John said.

"I went to the one on Eighth Street, off Columbus," Sarah said.

"I know it," Alan said.

"So does Kyle Erikson. That's where he transferred, right before the parties started in Vienna," John said.

"So he somehow found out I was donating there, transferred, stole my blood, and used it to make portals?" Sarah asked.

"Yeah, it looks that way," John said.

"Isn't it kind of dangerous to let a blood witch work at a blood donation facility?" Alan asked.

"Actually, it's kind of a good thing. They study blood their whole lives, they understand it better than any doctor. Some of them can even sense impurities. Only a Sanguimancer's blood can be used for blood magic, and only a Sanguimancer can successfully perform the rites. So as long as they aren't allowed to donate, there isn't a problem," John said, looking at Sarah.

"Do we know where this guy is?" Alan asked.

"That's where you come in. Call your station, and get an address for him. We know where he works, and we know his name. It shouldn't take long. In the meantime, were going back to Vienna," John said.

John told Sarah to stay put and the two detectives left.

CHAPTER 14

Once they were on the road, Alan called and got the address for Kyle Erikson.

"He lives just off Eighth Street, about a block from the Blood Center," Alan said.

"Not surprising. That blood donation place is probably the reason he moved in the first place," John said.

John's phone rang. He pulled it out of his pocket and answered it. There was a series of single syllable questions and answers, then he hung up.

"That was Springheel Jack. They're going to stop throwing the parties soon. One of the people he knows who goes to them overheard that they're getting too much heat, and they'll have to move out of Ohio," John said.

"So what do we know about this guy?" Alan asked.

"More than I'd like to, actually. He's been in and out of trouble since he was a kid. He could have been really good, he was a really talented Sanguimancer, but he got in with a bad crowd, got into drugs and petty crimes, ended up dropping out of high school. Eventually he straightened out enough to keep a steady job, but he was always on the radar, at least until he left town," John said.

"So he disappears to Vienna, getting himself off your radar. At the same time he gets a job at the same blood donation center Sarah Jackson goes to in Vienna and steals her blood to use in his portals for secret parties. Meaning he had to come back into Arcanum every time there was a party, and pray no one saw him making those portals," Alan said.

"Then he had to get everyone through, travel through himself, and when the party was over, drive back to Arcanum unseen and create another portal to get everyone back," John said.

"This sounds like a full time job," Alan said.

"Not only that, but Sarah's no fool. She would have been careful about who saw her and where she went in Vienna. Whoever told Erikson about her donating blood had to have a really good network to find her. Then they had to make sure that Erikson could get her blood," John said.

"This isn't just someone running underground no-rules parties," Alan said.

"No, whoever's running this is smart, connected, and has been planning ahead for at least a year to make all of this come together," John said. He stared out the windshield, his jaw set.

"What are we walking into, partner?" Alan asked.

"I don't know, but I'm glad I got you your gun back," John said.

"I'm going to call to get a warrant," Alan said, pulling his phone back out of his jacket.

"No, don't do that. We don't need a warrant," John said.

"If we're going to go in and arrest this guy, we're going to need some sort of official approval. If we just force our way in and search his place with no probable cause, it'll get thrown straight back out of court," Alan said.

"What law has he broken?" John asked.

"The... the thing with the portals and stealing the blood. Also the dead guy," Alan said.

"And you're going to call a judge in Vienna and ask him for an arrest warrant on a blood witch who stole another blood witch's blood and used it to make illegal portals between Arcanum and Vienna? How long do you think that phone call will last?" John asked.

"Probably not long enough to explain that I'm serious," Alan said. "So, what are we going to do? Head on over there, ask him politely if we might come in, then hit him with teddy bears until he confesses? Throw live wasps at him or something?" Alan asked.

"A witch's punishment for a witch's crime, Alan," John said.

CHAPTER 15

Half an hour later, they pulled up in front of the apartment building. It was a four-story brick building in the middle of the block with smaller buildings on either side. There were no signs that a dangerous witch lived here, or that anyone other than low income workers lived here, for that matter. Alan figured that so far he'd seen witches living in nice little bungalows, a super-jumping mutant making a living as a cat burglar, and a whole bunch of people living middle class lives while creating potions and blood magic in their spare time. So why not a criminal dark wizard living in a low income apartment in the middle of a midwestern city? Yeah, that made perfect sense.

"So this is where Kyle Erikson lives. I kinda expected something different," Alan said.

"Like what, a castle on a hill with flashes of lightning all around?" John said.

"Would that be so bad?" Alan said.

John stared into the middle distance again. He did that a lot, it was little off-putting.

"Actually, it would be *really* bad," he said, getting out of the SUV.

Alan figured no explanation could actually answer his questions about who might actually live in a castle on a hill surrounded by perpetual lightning or how John knew that someone living in such a place was worse than their current quarry, also that finding out that information wouldn't in any way help him in understanding exactly what had happened to the world, which only four days ago was full of drug addicts, pimps, wife beaters, and murderers. Now it was full of witches, demon-summoning occultists, fringe scientists, and mutants. Four days ago he was just a crazy guy, now he was a crazy guy with a gun, a badge, a dickhead coffeemaker/roommate, and a partner who might actually be a movie monster. As boring as it was, sometimes he kind of wished they'd left him on suspension.

The two men climbed the stairs to the fourth floor. Erikson's apartment was halfway down the hall. It was late in the evening. There wasn't anyone milling around in the hallway, though in buildings like this most of the tenants tended to keep to themselves.

The old, faded rug in the hall didn't quite reach the walls and was the kind of thing that most places would have pulled up years ago, and this place should have. As the two detectives made their way past the closed apartment doors, Alan kept waiting for little girls at the end of the hall to start asking him to play with them. Or maybe blood to pour out of the elevator. But there wasn't an elevator, this was only a four story building, and only buildings above five stories had to have elevators. It was a silly idea. Not the blood, at this point that seemed downright average. But a four story building with an elevator? Nah, never happen.

They finally got to Erikson's door without seeing a single man in a bear suit. John stood to one side, leaning his ear against the door to listen. Alan again saw the animal glimmer in his eyes. Alan had a thought that it had something to do with John using his senses, but there was no time to think on that now.

"He's in there," John mouthed.

Alan drew his gun and stepped back from the door. John did the same. Alan was waiting for John to try the knob, but apparently John had different plans. He stepped back from the door and fiercely kicked, stepping through as the frame splintered on both sides. Alan followed him in.

"Hello, Kyle," John said, cracking his neck.

The young man in the room stumbled backward, the plate of noodles he was holding falling with a clatter to the floor.

"Oh, *hell* no!" Erikson said, clawing his way out the open window.

"Fire escape!" John yelled. He crossed the room in a flash, but not fast enough. Erikson was already on the fire escape with the window closed. John was forcing the window up. Alan turned and ran back down the hall hoping to cut off Erikson before he made it down to the street.

Moments later Alan was on the street. He looked up at the fire escape and saw the worst case scenario: Erikson hadn't gone down the fire escape; he'd gone up it to the roof. John was close behind as Erikson topped the ladder and started to run to the right along the edge of the roof.

Something hit the ground by Alan's feet. The car keys. John had thrown them down as he got on the roof. Alan was jumping in the SUV as Kyle jumped over the alley to the next rooftop with John gaining on him at an incredible rate.

Alan started the truck and pulled out, hoping to get ahead of the action and cut off the chase. Erikson had made it to another rooftop now, and John was about to make the jump. Alan could just see them over the edge of the roofline as he caught up.

John jumped, just steps behind Erikson now. Alan saw a strange, human-shaped shimmer appear on the roof in front of John. It almost twinkled in the darkness, a semi-transparent silhouette against the starless sky. At that moment, John stopped in midair. He was held there, hovering over the alley like a ragdoll floating in space.

Alan had a bad feeling that he knew what was coming next. He slammed on the brakes of John's SUV and slid it into the alley, skidding to a halt just under where John was hanging. Seconds later there was a loud thud above him as the roof of the truck partially caved in. John rolled down the windshield and off the front of the SUV. As Alan stepped out to check on him, John yelled.

"He's climbing down the fire escape on the other side!" he howled, holding his right arm.

Alan bolted from the alley on foot. He came around the building in seconds and saw Erikson standing facing the wall, a strange light illuminating his features. He didn't slow down. He kept running. Erikson was stepping through the portal when Alan hit him at the waist, knocking them both to the ground.

Alan landed on top. A full-sprint tackle wasn't usually his forte, but it worked. He'd knocked the wind out of Erikson, and the man lay on the ground, gasping for breath as Alan cuffed his hands behind his back. He dragged the witch back to the car to find John leaning up against it in obvious pain.

John and Kyle stared at each other for a moment. John smiled. A slight smile with no hint of joy in it. It was a smile you'd expect from a panther. A predator that'd finally cornered its prey. Alan was starting to think maybe his partner was actually a vampire.

CHAPTER 15

Back at the Vienna Police station, Kyle Erikson was sitting stewing in an interrogation room. He hadn't actually committed a crime in Vienna, so Alan told the chief that he ran when they tried to question him, and assaulted Detective Weatherby. John seemed like his pride was a little hurt by this, but it was easier than explaining what had actually happened. Alan was too damn tired to answer stupid questions tonight.

Alan was watching Erikson through the two way mirror when John walked in, his right arm in a sling.

"How bad?" Alan asked.

"Dislocated elbow, nothing that won't heal," John said.

"That must hurt like hell," Alan said, fighting the urge to poke it like a fresh tattoo.

"Not as bad as he's going to be hurting," John said. "Has he said anything yet?"

"Haven't talked to him," Alan said, "I figured I'd wait for you."

John looked at him and smiled. It wasn't a predatory smile, just an honest, friendly one.

"Thanks for that," he said.

"He looks nervous," Alan said.

"He should be," John responded.

The two detectives walked out of the observation room and into the interrogation room. Alan looked at the young man, his wrists still handcuffed, with the cuffs looped through a steel bar in the table. He was in his twenties. Alan thought he looked as though someone stretched his skin too tight over his bones, at least on his face. It was either a horrible face lift or some kind of disgusting latex mask on a skeleton. He looked like his eyes were about to pop out of his head. Alan couldn't decide if this was out of fear, some kind of magical exhaustion, or years of drug use. He never would have pegged this guy for a dangerous witch. More likely a slightly less dangerous street addict.

"You can't keep me here," he said, looking at Alan. "You don't understand; it's not safe for me here."

"Kyle, look at my partner and ask me again if I know how much danger you're in," Alan said, sitting down across the table from Erikson. John took the chair next to Alan.

"He doesn't know either. Detective Weatherby, I need to go back to Arcanum. It really isn't safe for me here," Erikson said.

"You know what's waiting for you in Arcanum," John said.

"Yeah, a trial. They might lock me up; they might burn me at the stake. But if he knows you caught me, it will be so much worse, man. So much worse!" Erikson said.

He really sounded like a junkie now, full-on Tinfoil Hat Society. There was no doubting this guy had a drug problem, and he made Alan look calm with his paranoia.

"Who is he, Kyle? You tell us who's running the parties, and maybe we'll transfer you to Arcanum and lock you up there," John said.

"I can't tell you. I really can't tell you. If he even thinks I'm going to mention his name, I'm worse than dead, Weatherby," Erikson said.

Alan watched his face. He had a little bit of spit at the corners of his lips as he talked even though his lips themselves were dry and cracked. He looked like a zombie, or a particularly lively corpse. Alan wondered as he watched the man babble if those two things were actually the same thing or different things that in his brain were one thing. Also, why was he saying *thing* so much? Alan tuned back in. John was still playing hardball.

"I have to go back to Arcanum!" Erikson said.

"You're not going anywhere until we have a name. You give us that, and we'll take you back there tonight. I'll tell my boss we're coming and you'll have full protection right up until I light the match that burns you to death," John said.

Alan wasn't sure if he was just being morbid or was actually serious. It was probably best to just assume that morbid *was* serious.

"Look, Kyle," Alan said. "I can't begin to understand how scared you are, or who you're afraid of.

In my brain he's kind of a cross between Cthulhu and Charlie Brown. Also probably a pretty bad dancer."

Erikson stared at Alan. John stared at Alan.

"Okay, so my point is this: We're not afraid of him. And we're not afraid of you. And I'm not afraid of your weird Council. Tell us what we need to know and we'll make sure you make it to your fiery death in one piece," Alan said.

Was this what police work was now, since the robots had taken over? Was the best he could offer a criminal who had stolen blood to make magical portals a safe trip to a pyre? Also, he was questioning a man who was making magical portals with stolen blood. Because of a man who had been turned into jelly. Somehow that didn't seem weird anymore. In fact, that was the most normal thing about his life now. What had happened to Aaron Burroughs, anyway?

"Hey Kyle, let's change direction for a minute here," Alan said, interrupting the skull-face-mask talking hole again.

Erikson looked at him, getting visibly more desperate with every passing moment.

"What happened to Aaron Burroughs?" Alan asked.

Erikson seemed relieved to change the subject.

"He told me to make the physicist fall. He was asking questions," Erikson said. "He wanted to get in, but he was asking too many questions."

"Questions about what?" John asked.

"Who went, who could get in, who was doing what," Erikson said.

"I'm more interested in how he got turned into a disgusting lemon-flavored jello mold, Kyle," Alan said.

"What?" Erikson said. He cocked his head in the way Alan was getting used to since coming back to work. "How do you know he's lemon-flavored?"

"What happened to him, Kyle?" John said.

"All I did was change the destination of the portal. It was supposed to look like he jumped. When I heard what happened, I checked my work. Nothing I did could do that," Erikson said.

"What could?" Alan asked.

"It had to be the radiation. That's the only thing that could do it. Something about the radiation he was working with must have changed his molecular structure. When he went through the portal, well..." Erikson said.

"I'm still not getting it," Alan said.

"Going through a portal effects your molecules. Not permanently, but for the duration of the journey," John said.

"So, if his body was already screwed up from the alchemy experiments the portal just made it worse," Alan said.

"If I'd known what was going to happen, I would have sent him into a river or something. If he'd just looked like a jumper, I wouldn't be here right now," Erikson said.

"Who is this guy we're dealing with, Kyle? Why is he throwing these parties?" John asked.

"Parties? Oh man, you've got it all wrong," Erikson said.

"What are they, then?" Alan asked.

"He's looking for people; he's putting together a network," Erikson said.

"A network of witches? Why is he doing that?" John asked.

"I really don't know. He only tells me what I need to know. He's the same way with everyone. He keeps information to himself and only tells the people what to do when it's time to do it. Everything goes through him. What I can tell you is whatever he's trying to do, it's dark. Like, really dark. We're talking real blackblood shit, Weatherby," Erikson said.

John tensed a bit at that word.

"So who is he? Or should I just go back to Arcanum and tell everyone how helpful you're being while you sit in a jail cell here, completely vulnerable?" John asked.

"You can't do that, Weatherby. You know you can't!" Erikson pleaded.

"Why can't I? We know you've been stealing blood from the blood bank. We can prove that, or at least hold you for it. In the meantime, I can drive back to Arcanum and report to the Council."

"Okay. I'll tell you his name. You promise to get me out of here right now, and I'll tell you," Erikson said.

The air in the room felt strange. Alan could feel it, but no one else seemed to. It was almost electric, like static in the air.

"Tell us his name, Kyle," John said.

John stopped, looking around. He seemed to be sniffing the air. He stood up, kicking back his chair and crossing to the other side of the table as a black fog formed behind Erikson. John tried to uncuff him.

The black fog condensed in less than a second into the shape of a man. Alan drew his gun and fired as the black shape grabbed Erikson and began to disappear. Alan thought he saw the man in the fog recoil from one of the gunshots as John grabbed at the screaming Erikson, but he vanished with the cloud, leaving the still-locked handcuffs on the table.

"Shit!" John screamed, slamming his good fist into the wall.

"I think I hit it," Alan said, the barrel of his gun still smoking.

Five cops came charging into the room, guns drawn to find Alan staring at a chair and John silently fuming, his fist still buried in the wall.

CHAPTER 16

The next day, John dropped Alan off in front of the Darke County Archive. John was headed to Sarah's house to explain what had happened, and to warn her that there might be more trouble coming. Alan thought he might also be trying to make amends for accusing her of breaking her promise. He figured he'd let John handle that one on his own, he had no particular interest in getting involved in a possible-vampire and confirmed witch personal drama. Besides, he had business of his own.   He had enough trouble just trying to keep his coffeemaker happy and figure out who the woman was that left lipstick in his bathroom.

Something had been bothering him about the night before.   Actually, a lot of things were bothering him, especially the part where a person made up of self-forming black clouds stole a suspect out of an interrogation room in his police station.   That part really bothered him.   So did the part where he was told he'd have to pay for the bullet holes he'd put in the wall trying to shoot the cloud-man.   He had to explain the cloud-man to Captain Clark, which was difficult.   Difficult like trying to explain that you were shooting at a cloud that spontaneously formed in the middle of an interrogation and stole your suspect.

But that wasn't why he was at the Archive.   He was thinking about that genealogy book Doctor Alighieri had shown him.   It listed the families and their respective specialties in magic.   Whoever had stopped John in midair could appear out of nothing, disguise themselves by making a weird shimmer, and levitate someone.   Alan was taking a stab in the dark that a combination of abilities like that might be unusual. He had no idea if it was, or even if he could describe what he'd actually seen. But it was worth a try.

He knocked on the door and Alighieri answered almost immediately.

"Detective Schriever, so *nice* to see you again!" he said, shaking Alan's hand.

"Hello, Doctor. I was wondering if you could help me with something." Alan said.

"Of course, my boy. Is this for the case?" Alighieri asked.

"Sort of. We actually found who was making the portals, but he was taken in the middle of our interrogation. We think whoever is running the meetings took him to keep him from talking," Alan said.

"Oh, that's good," Alighieri said.

Alan looked at him. He finally got to use that quizzical look that everyone had been using on him lately.

"Oh, that Sarah wasn't involved," Alighieri specified.

"Ahh," Alan said, "yes, it is. John is out talking to her now. Actually, while we were trying to catch the man, something strange happened to John. That's what I'd like to talk to you about."

Alighieri's face went stern. He suddenly looked like an angered headmaster. At least Alan thought he did. He'd gone to public school. They didn't have headmasters at his school. They had an armed security guard and metal detectors, though.

"If you want to know something about Detective Weatherby, I'm afraid you're going to have to ask him directly. His family is one about which I will share no details," Alighieri said.

"Oh, no, Doctor. It's not about him. He was injured last night by a glimmering cloud person that made him float over an alley," Alan said.

Why didn't it feel awkward to utter that out loud?

"Oh my, well that is a different thing. You said the glimmering cloud made him levitate? How, exactly? I must know the circumstances," Alighieri asked. His eyes narrowed as he spoke, like he'd just heard that someone had cheated a child.

"He was chasing Erikson across rooftops. As he jumped from one to the next, the shimmery cloud appeared on the roof in front of him and stopped him in midair," Alan said.

"Oh, forced levitation. That is a difficult skill," Alighieri said.

"That's what I was hoping," Alan said. "That genealogy book you showed my when we were here lists abilities as they pass through families. I was hoping we might narrow down who may have done it."

"Oh, I think we can do just that," Alighieri said, hopping slightly.

He seemed strangely and honestly excited about his little moment of detective work. Alan didn't know if it was because he had a boring job or he wanted to help catch someone who hurt John. Alan couldn't imagine being both a witch and the historian for a town as weird as this one could ever be boring.

Alighieri led him into the Archive. As they passed through the doorway, Alan thought about the security system.

"What exactly happens if you aren't supposed to be in here and you try to come in?" he asked.

"I told you this last time you were here, my boy," Alighieri said, "you die."

It was matter of fact, offhand, and incredibly disturbing. There was no sense of concern about it, no sense of pride, either. Just the knowledge that it worked. Also, no further explanation.

Alighieri pulled the book off its plinth and moved it to a nearby table. He opened it to the first page and started scanning with his finger, muttering to himself as he went along. After a few moments, he glanced up at Alan.

"You said that he was stopped in midair?" he asked.

"Yes. He was jumping, and he just stopped. Is that important?" Alan asked.

"Well, there are two types of levitation," Alighieri said. "The first one is the denial of gravity." He said, pointing to a family line. "If that had been used, he would have continued moving forward, he would have kept your momentum, you see. That's this family, the Guenther line. They're early settlers, a Germanic people. I don't think there are any actual people named Guenther left in town, actually. They had a lot of girls."

"And what about the other type?" Alan asked.

"Oh, that one is more common, mostly over here," Alighieri said, flipping a few pages and pointing to names as he went. "What they can do is actually create a force against gravity."

"Like a jet pack?" Alan asked.

"Actually, a bit, yes. It is an easier technique, and like I said more common. But it is still limited to a few families. Unfortunately, they're some of the original families, and are quite large groups by now. Thousands of them roaming around," Alighieri said.

"So a suspect pool of several thousand," Alan said. "That's not very helpful."

"No, but you said that the person appeared on the roof and was shimmering?" Alighieri asked.

"Yes. They just kind of formed there, in exactly the way a person shouldn't," Alan said.

"Tell me about the shimmering," Alighieri said.

"It was a shimmering person on a rooftop in the middle of a police chase. It was bright, kind of see-through, multicolored, and also, it was a shimmering person," Alan said.

"Ahh, you're more help than you think, Detective. You said it appeared there. That's transportation. More details would help, but not everyone can teleport into open space like that, that narrows it down," Alighieri said.

"I'm glad I could help?" Alan said.

Alighieri smiled. "Now, the shimmering was clearly a shrouding spell," he said.

"Clearly." Alan agreed, having no idea what he was agreeing to.

"That is yet another uncommon talent. Let's see where our three threads meet, shall we?" Alighieri said.

He flipped back and forth between pages, checking and rechecking names and details. He muttered to himself the whole time. He would stop and point to a name, make a verbal note of it, and then turn to another page and repeat the process, confirming or disproving some connection. This went on at a steady pace for several minutes. Alan was a little bit disappointed that there wasn't some kind of magic spell to make these connections, or at least a computer or card catalogue.

"There!" Alighieri exclaimed, pointing to a name deep in the book. This is the family line where all of those abilities intersect."

"Great! Where does that leave us?" Alan said.

"Well, they intersect in the early twentieth century, so the group is still pretty big, but, wait, no," Alighieri stopped and stared at the page for a moment.

"What's wrong?" Alan asked, looking over his shoulder.

"There's a family missing. Someone has removed them from the book," Alighieri said. His tone was both frightened and angry.

"Why would they do that?" Alan asked.

"*Why* isn't the question. The real question is *how*. This is a magic book. The information isn't written in by hand, it is added through a spell that's older than me," Alighieri said.

"What family is it?" Alan asked.

"Let's see, it's an old family, the only living relative is Adrienne Marks, married to Paul Cooper." Alighieri said.

"Adrienne Cooper. As in the woman on the Council who tried to block John and I from getting access to the Archive. Could she have erased the information?" Alan asked.

"I suppose she could have, but I don't know why. No one ever looks in here. The book only exists to track the growth and spread of the families in Darke County, and the people that are missing aren't ever residents. The family member who links them moved away forty years ago." Alighieri said.

"Doctor," Alan said, "is Adrienne Cooper capable of the transportation, shrouding spell, and forced levitation?"

"Yes, they're all family abilities she has inherited," Alighieri said.

"Is she capable of removing information from the genealogy?" Alan asked.

"Well, several of her ancestors were founders; they're the ones who created the spell, so she'd be blood bound to it. I suppose if she managed to find out how it was created, she could affect it. But why would she?" Alighieri said.

"She's hiding something, protecting someone. I can't tell you who or what yet, but I can tell you that I plan to find out." Alan said.

Alighieri just looked at him for a moment as though wondering what to say.

"Doctor, I need you to keep this to yourself. The possible connection to what happened to John, the missing information, Burroughs' death, all of it. Something dark is going on here, and I'd prefer it if you didn't tell anyone that you know about this, let me handle it for now," Alan said.

Alighieri nodded. "My boy, I am the keeper of Archives and secrets, I've been doing it a long time, and I assure you I can do it a while longer. If there's something foul afoot, I'll keep it quiet until you tell me otherwise," he said.

"Thank you, Doctor," Alan said.   He shook Alighieri's hand and left the Archive.

CHAPTER 17

John was leaning against the SUV when Alan came through the doors. He looked every bit like a nineteen fifties gangster. His dark grey suit was buttoned even though the sun was beating down, his black shoes were so polished they glimmered. Wayfarer sunglasses hid his eyes; Alan hadn't seen him with them off in the sun. His impossibly perfect dark hair was still impossibly perfect. His mouth was set in a hard straight line that cut across his face like a razor.

"How did it go?" Alan asked.

John shrugged, pushing himself off the truck. "As well as it could," he said. "Did you find out what you wanted with Alighieri?"

"Yeah, I did. And I think we should talk about it. I was investigating who stopped you on the roof last night," Alan said.

"What did you find out?" John asked.

"Alighieri helped me look up who had all the abilities necessary to do it. We narrowed it down to a family. It's the Marks family. Adrienne Cooper was born a Marks," Alan said.

"The same Adrienne Cooper who attacked me in the Council Chamber and tried to stop us getting into the Archive in the first place," John said, looking across at the City Hall.

"The same one. She's protecting someone. There's a whole family related to hers missing from the genealogy. Alighieri said that only someone from a founding family could possibly have done it," Alan said.

"Interesting," John said. "I wonder who she's protecting. Family ties run pretty strong here, and especially with the founding families. Very few of them would hesitate to break the law to protect family, but there's usually nothing we can do about it. Council Members are more or less untouchable. The only exception is if they're convicted of black magic. That's still an offense punished by immolation or banishment, even for them. Whatever she's covering up must be very serious to go to these lengths," John said, still looking at the City Hall. There was a commotion there now; a group of women were walking down the front steps. "We can't go after her, anyway. She's on the Council," he said.

Alan was looking at the City Hall now. He saw the Council members walking down the steps.

"You live here. You work here. They're untouchable to you. To me, she's just a woman who tried to kill my partner," Alan said.

Before John could say anything, Alan jogged across the street. The group of women was breaking up, headed in different directions. He picked Adrienne Cooper out of the people milling on the sidewalk. It took him a few moments to catch up.

"Adrienne Cooper," he called out.

She stopped and turned around.

"Detective Schriever. I hear you found the solution to the mystery of our dead citizen," she said.

Alan stepped up close to her on the sidewalk. "Yes, we did. Unfortunately, Detective Weatherby was injured in catching the man. The suspect was kidnapped from our interrogation by a black cloud, so we didn't get any good information," Alan said.

"Oh, I'm sorry to hear that. If there's something illicit going on in our town, we certainly want to stop it," Adrienne Cooper said.

"See, that's what's interesting to me. I don't really think you do," Alan said, stepping forward.

"I don't understand," Cooper said.

"Well, I did a little research. I know there are only a few people in town that could have done that to John. And strangely, you're on that list. The only person who in any way tried to hinder our investigation is one of the few capable of what happened," Alan said.

"You think I injured Detective Weatherby? You're crazy," Cooper said.

"I am crazy. Very crazy, and way more dangerous than I seem. What I'm not is stupid. I will find out what's going on and who's behind it, and what connection they have to you. If anything happens to John, to me, to anyone either of us cares about, whether I can prove it was you or not, there isn't enough magic in the world to protect you from what I'm capable of. Do we understand each other?" Alan said, nearly hissing in her face.

"You have no idea who you're dealing with, Detective," Adrienne hissed back.

"Neither do you, witch," Alan growled.

He walked back to John, who was still standing by the SUV.

"She watched you walk all the way back," John said. "What the hell did you say to her?"

"Nothing much, I just reminded her that I'm a recently-freed mental patient with a gun, and she can't outrun bullets," Alan said, smiling.

"Good Lord. That's going to be a hell storm," John said, getting in the SUV.

Alan got in the passenger side.

"I hope it is. Maybe my crazy will rattle her enough to make her trip up and lead us to whoever is running this thing," Alan said.

"Hopefully that will happen before we both end up like Erikson," John said, starting the engine.

They drove back to Vienna to finalize what promised to be the most confusing and false incident report he'd ever written.

CHAPTER 18

"There won't be an incident report," Captain Clark said. "The government came in and took everything. They took the body, the reports, the computers, the surveillance footage. They even took the damn bullets out of the wall."

John and Alan had barely made it through the door before a uniform told them that the Captain wanted to see them. He'd looked very disturbed. Alan thought he may have been trying to overcome his programming, or possibly had a bad burrito. The burrito thing was still an option.

"Okay. So what do we do now?" Alan asked.

"You ruined this case, Schriever. You lost the suspect, fired your weapon in the station at nothing, and we have no answers after all that. I should fire you right now."

"Captain," John interrupted, "You can't blame Detective Schriever for what happened. The situation was unavoidable."

There was a strange tone in his voice. Alan hadn't heard him talk like that before. It was soothing, but with a strange, monotonous ringing in it.

"I'd love to fire you, but I can't," Clark said. He gestured out the door behind them.

A woman walked in. She was in her late fifties. Short, but well-built and healthy. She looked like she'd seen a fight or two in her life. Also like she'd never lost one.

"Who's that?" Alan asked John.

"The Sheriff of Darke County," John said.

"Who?" Alan said.

"My boss," John said.

"Oh," Alan said.

"We've decided," she said, stepping over next to Captain Clark, "because the strange events of the past week that there should be a joint task force between Darke County and Vienna to investigate cross-border crimes."

"That sounds like a good plan, sir," John said. "Might I suggest…"

"The Captain and I have already decided that you and Detective Schriever will be the principle agents on the task force," The Sheriff said, interrupting John.

"How do you feel about this, Captain?" Alan asked.

"I think it is a terrible idea. I think that you're the worst possible choice for any type of police work," Captain Clark said. "But I don't have any choice in the matter. This comes from over my head."

"Way over your head, Captain. Don't forget that," The Sheriff said.

"We're giving you an office in the basement. You'll have your own computer system, linked to our databases but separate, and the resources of both departments at your disposal," Captain Clark said, his voice sounded defeated and intimidated.

Alan wondered how far over his head they'd had to go to get approval for this.

"Here's the keys to the office. Basement Level, first door to the right off the elevator. Darke County has already set up your computer systems and phones," The Captain said, holding out the keys.

Alan took the keys from his hand, trying to not the mischievous grin get too wide.

"You're both dismissed. Get down to your office and set up," the Sheriff said.

"Schriever," Captain Clark said as they reached the door.

Alan stopped and turned.

"Don't forget; I'm still your boss," Clark said.

"Gotcha, Captain," Alan said, throwing a salute. "And I still think you might be a robot," Alan smiled as he walked out of the bullpen. He could almost feel Captain Clark's internal scream on his back.

The office in the basement wasn't fancy, but it would do. A couple of desks, some whiteboards, and the rest of the essentials. Everything a cop needs.

John sat down at one of the desks and opened a drawer. He pulled a brand new laptop out of it.

"Standard issue," he said, opening it up and typing.

"Not in this station, it's not," Alan said. He checked the other desk. There was a laptop in the drawer of his, as well. There were also several pieces of equipment he didn't immediately recognize.

"I'm exhausted. I think I'll have to figure out the rest of this tomorrow," Alan said. "You going to stick around and work?"

"I think I am. I have a report to write, and there're a few things I want to go over," John said without looking up from the screen.

"Okay," Alan said.

He walked over to John and shook his hand. As he passed John's desk, he saw the confiscated security footage from the interrogation room on the screen. John had the section where the cloud appeared running on a loop in full screen, scrutinizing it.

"Tomorrow, then," Alan said, walking out of the office.

"Tomorrow," John said.   He was still staring at the screen.

Alan knew John definitely wasn't a robot.   Now on to that coffeemaker.